SECRETS OF THE
CASTLETON
MANOR LIBRARY™

A Thorny Plot

Catherine Dilts

Annie's®
AnniesFiction.com

Books in the Secrets of the Castleton Manor Library series

A Novel Murder
Bitter Words
The Grim Reader
A Deadly Chapter
An Autographed Mystery
Second Edition Death
A Crime Well Versed
A Murder Unscripted
Pride and Publishing
A Literary Offense
Up to Noir Good
For Letter or Worse
On Pens and Needles
Ink or Swim
Tell No Tales
Page Fright
A Fatal Yarn
Read Between the Crimes
From Fable to Grave
A Fateful Sentence
Cloak and Grammar
A Lost Clause
A Thorny Plot
A Scary Tale Wedding

A Thorny Plot
Copyright © 2019, 2023 Annie's.

All rights reserved. No part of this publication may be reproduced, stored in a retrieval system, or transmitted in any form or by any means—electronic, mechanical, photocopying, recording or otherwise—without the prior written permission of the publisher. The only exception is brief quotations in printed reviews. For information address Annie's, 306 East Parr Road, Berne, Indiana 46711-1138.

The characters and events in this book are fictional, and any resemblance to actual persons or events is coincidental.

Library of Congress-in-Publication Data
A Thorny Plot / by Catherine Dilts
p. cm.
I. Title
2018966412

AnniesFiction.com
(800) 282-6643
Secrets of the Castleton Manor Library™
Series Creator: Shari Lohner
Series Editor: Lorie Jones
Cover Illustrator: Jesse Reisch

10 11 12 13 14 | Printed in China | 9 8 7

1

The garden at Castleton Manor featured a stunning variety of dahlias, from cheery pink blossoms to sunset-hued blooms the size of dinner plates. A fountain splashed in the midst of lush foliage. Librarian Faith Newberry inhaled the perfume of flowers, grateful that she worked in such a beautiful setting.

Gardening enthusiasts, authors of gardening-themed mystery novels, and well-known horticulturists had descended on Castleton Manor in Lighthouse Bay, Massachusetts, for the six-day Hidden Treasures Literary and Gardening Retreat based on the children's classic *The Secret Garden* by Frances Hodgson Burnett. The manor had been chosen as the venue in part because of its amazing flower, vegetable, and herb gardens.

The opening discussion was scheduled to begin in an hour. It was appropriately set in one of the many gardens surrounding the manor, where the flower beds were an explosion of colors.

One of the workmen approached Faith. "Where do you want the podium?"

"Let's find Ms. Russell," Faith answered. "She has the plan."

The perpetually organized Marlene Russell held a clipboard as she directed the arrangement of chairs and round café tables on an expanse of perfectly trimmed lawn. The assistant manager wore a linen suit in a soft green that matched her eyes.

"Does the podium go by the fountain or the bench?" Faith asked her.

"The bench." Marlene smoothed a stray strand of wavy blonde hair tousled by the light breeze. "I do hope the weather continues to be mild this week. The event organizers insist we hold most of the sessions outdoors, given the nature of the retreat."

"I'm sure everything will be fine," Faith said.

"That's because you're an optimist," Marlene told her. She faced the workman who had followed Faith. "The podium can come this way."

Faith realized she wasn't needed and walked across the grass to greet her friend Brooke Milner, the manor's head chef, who was putting the finishing touches on the buffet table.

Brooke saw her and smiled. "Your outfit is cute."

"Thanks. I knew we'd be outside in this August heat, so I wanted something that would breathe well." Faith wore a flowy dress with a print of large lavender roses and a short-sleeved cardigan. She had opted for dressy low-heeled sandals, which were more practical for walking on the grass and garden paths. Her long chestnut hair was pulled back with a clip.

"Don't get me wrong," Brooke continued. "I love my job, but the wardrobe is boring." She motioned to her work uniform of a white chef's jacket and black pants.

"Do you need a hand with the food?"

"I'm almost finished." Brooke stepped back. "What do you think?"

Faith regarded the elegant table topped with a white linen cloth. Plates, utensils, napkins, and crystal glassware sat on one end. On the other were chafing dishes filled with savory hot breakfast foods and cloches that covered pastries and fresh fruit. Two vases held edible flowers for adventurous diners.

"It's hard to compete with the natural beauty of the garden," Faith said, "but you've managed to pull it off. This table should be on the cover of a gourmet magazine."

Brooke beamed. "Thank you. I hope our guests will agree with you."

"Hello, Faith!" called a familiar voice.

She whirled around to see her parents, Martin and Barbara Newberry, striding toward her across the lawn. Both looked ready for an elegant garden party. Her mother's shoulder-length blonde hair, streaked with silver, was topped with a stylish straw hat. The hatband matched her poppy-print sundress. Her father was tall and broad, with a twinkle in his eye. His khakis and short-sleeved silk shirt were surprisingly fashionable. She suspected Mom had convinced him to get a wardrobe makeover, at least for the duration of the retreat.

Faith hugged her parents. "I'm so glad you made it in time for the opening talk."

"We were long overdue for a visit," her mother said. "I'm glad we also get the chance to see Lionel Foille in person. Oh, don't try to put a French pronunciation on his name."

"Marlene already warned us," Brooke said with a smile. "She said it's pronounced like 'aluminum foil' but without the aluminum."

"We're faithful viewers of his television program," her father remarked.

Faith laughed. "You and a million other gardeners." She checked her watch. It was a few minutes past eight, and they were nearly ready. "The retreat begins in less than an hour."

"Great," her dad said. "That will give us time to unload the car."

Watson, Faith's black-and-white tuxedo cat with a stubby tail, wound around her mother's ankles, purring.

Her mom reached down to scratch behind his ears. "It's good to see you too. How's my favorite kitty?" She straightened and turned to Faith. "Seriously, how is he doing? Companion animals often have difficulty accepting changes in their caretaker's routine. Especially something as life changing as an engagement."

Faith's mother had a deep concern for the well-being of animals. She regularly played foster mom to cats and dogs in need of care.

"I haven't been able to spend as much alone time with Watson as I'd like, but he seems to be doing all right." Faith removed a key from her cardigan pocket. "This is your key to the cottage for the week. The guest room is ready. You can park next to my car."

Part of the compensation for her employment as librarian was free lodging in the old gardener's cottage on the grounds. She'd insisted on her parents staying with her during the retreat.

"Good," her mother said. "I'd like to freshen up and get settled."

Faith thought her mother already looked terrific. Both her parents seemed rested, despite rising early to drive here from their home in Springfield, Massachusetts.

Faith also suspected that while the gardening retreat was their excuse, their primary goal in attending was getting to know her fiancé, Wolfe Jaxon—who co-owned the manor—and his family better before their wedding in September.

For a moment, the cat considered following his human's parents to the cottage, but things were more interesting here. The garden was buzzing with activity and not just from the honeybees lazily circling the flowers. He hopped onto a chair and settled in to watch.

A fresh crop of guests trickled into the garden, followed by their humans. Castleton Manor welcomed people, but more importantly, their animal companions. The cat was pleased to see a variety of felines and small dogs. Introductions could wait, though. For now, he was content to soak up the sunshine and observe.

The peaceful summer morning was disturbed by a sudden commotion. Humans grabbed their furry companions and exclaimed loudly with many noises when a simple bark or meow would have sufficed.

The cat stood on his chair, ready to run.

A reddish creature with pointy ears and a curly tail raced into the garden. It careened into the cat's perch, nearly tipping over the chair.

He felt his fur puff in an involuntary reaction. How undignified.

"Fox!" *a human yelled.*

The cat glared after the creature. No, this animal might resemble a fox, but he had none of the finesse of the woodland hunters. In fact, the animal had the bumbling enthusiasm of the most ridiculous of canines.

He had come to tolerate dogs quite well, but this fellow had a wild streak he would prefer to avoid.

"I'm so sorry!" a woman cried as she dashed into the garden. She appeared to be in her early forties, with a trim athletic build and short brown hair, but her features were careworn, as though she'd endured a good deal of stress. The woman grabbed the animal's leash. "Reynard, you naughty boy."

Faith recognized Lois Girten from the retreat program. She was the author of a cozy mystery series whose main character was a gardener, and she was scheduled to give several talks.

Marlene crossed her arms and frowned. "Wild animals are not allowed in the manor."

Although the manor had a pet-friendly policy, Marlene did not approve of animals having the run of the luxurious mansion. Misbehavior provided an excuse to ban them. Faith knew this from experience. Watson had been temporarily banned on more than one occasion.

"He's perfectly domesticated, only excited." Lois glanced around at the startled guests. "Reynard is not a fox. He's a Shiba Inu. I assure you that he's a dog."

"You must retain control of him if you expect to keep him at the manor," Marlene said sternly.

Faith noticed other guests nodding in agreement as they cradled their pets in their arms. She glanced around for Watson.

The cat had trotted up to a woman in a sporty red wheelchair. The wide, nubby tires enabled her to wheel around the lawn with no difficulty.

The woman had thick brown hair, and her bright smile seemed to tell the world nothing was going to hold her back. When she reached down to pet Watson, he stood on his hind legs, sniffing her chair. The woman patted the light blanket covering her lap, and Watson gently jumped up.

Faith smiled. Watson was already making a new friend. The retreat was beginning soon, so she'd have to meet the woman later. She returned her attention to the conversation.

Lois was still apologizing.

Even though Reynard wagged his curlicue tail and gazed adoringly at Marlene, the assistant manager wore a stern expression. She was generally immune to the wiles of cute pets, although Watson had managed to charm her once or twice.

"Just make certain it doesn't happen again," Marlene said finally.

Faith breathed a sigh of relief. The retreat could begin without further complications. Or so she hoped.

"You must be kidding," a large man griped. He held a tiny Pomeranian. The dog's fur was a patchwork quilt of black and gray-blue colors. It could have passed for an adorable stuffed toy. The man's hair shared the pup's coloring, with a fringe of gray-streaked black circling his bald dome.

Faith had seen the man's photo in the retreat program too, but she already knew him from his popular television show. Lionel Foille was a gardening celebrity.

"For one thing," Lionel continued, facing Marlene, "that creature could cause serious harm to my Patches. For another, what evidence do we have that it isn't a fox? Lois Girten is infamous for her shoddy research. The woman's every word is suspect. I will not have my dog's life put at risk to suit her whims."

Lois's stunned expression was slowly overtaken by a frown. "Well, well, the mighty Lionel Foille comes striding into the retreat with a bloody scythe in his fist, ready to mow down anyone who disagrees with him."

The author's vivid imagery made Faith a little queasy.

Brooke sidled up to Faith. "And I thought gardening enthusiasts would be a peaceful bunch," she whispered. "The retreat hasn't even started, and they're already at each other's throats."

"This is not a matter for discussion," Lionel huffed. "I am clearly in the right to request your so-called dog's immediate expulsion from the premises."

Lois's face flushed red. "I was invited here, and I'm part of the program. You didn't manage to completely destroy my career with your bad reviews. What do you have against me, anyway?"

"I merely seek to prevent unwitting readers from consuming your drivel." Lionel snorted. "In your third novel, you had pansies bloom in August." He waved a hand. "Do you see any pansies here? No, because they bloom in the spring and fall. And in your fourth novel—"

"Which could have been my last, thanks to you." Lois clenched her free hand into a fist. "You couldn't grow a turnip without the aid of your team of professional gardeners."

As their owners' voices rose, the Shiba Inu danced on his hind legs, jerking against the leash, and the tiny Pomeranian yipped.

Guests listened in on the argument with obvious interest.

"Please calm down." Marlene held her hands up and stepped between Lionel and Lois. "We need to get ready for the program. It begins in less than an hour."

A woman rushed to Marlene's aid, negotiating the groomed lawn in high heels. She was stunning in a knee-length, cool-blue dress that complemented her dark complexion. A silk scarf was wrapped around her hair, which was a mass of lustrous black curls. "Mr. Foille, I was wondering if you would be willing to do an impromptu book signing before we kick off the event."

"What a lovely idea," Marlene broke in before Lionel could reply. "And, Ms. Girten, why don't you sit over here and do the same?"

Marlene steered Lois in one direction, and the woman led Lionel to a round café table on the opposite side of the garden. Both speakers were soon busy autographing books for fans.

Marlene and the woman returned to the podium, where Faith and Brooke waited.

Marlene made introductions. "This is Rose Fairwell, the retreat director. Rose, our librarian, Faith Newberry, and head chef, Brooke Milner."

After shaking hands with Faith and Brooke, Rose said quietly, "I knew I was taking my chances inviting them both to the same event. But I thought their old dustup was water under the bridge."

"You expected them to act professionally," Marlene said. "No one will blame you for that undignified little spat."

"Why would Lionel review a novel?" Faith asked. "He's a gardening expert, not a literary critic."

"He must have decided to read it for pleasure," Rose said. "Lois made one little mistake in a book, and it became his mission to point out every gardening error in her series."

"Lois's books are fiction," Brooke said. "What's the big deal?"

"Lionel must not understand the concept of literary license." Rose sighed. "I can see I'll be playing referee for the entire retreat."

A retreat Rose had worked for months to organize. Faith felt for her. "Please let me know if there's anything I can do to help."

Rose smiled. "I'll keep that in mind."

Guests settled at the café tables, examining their program guides. Animal companions relaxed. The atmosphere was soon calm and peaceful.

Until a young man burst into the garden. He wore a polo shirt with a television news logo printed on the left breast pocket. Following close behind was a woman in a matching shirt, hefting a video camera.

"Are we late?" the young man asked.

The woman scanned the area. "Where can I set up my camera?"

"Excuse me," Marlene said. "May I see your passes?"

"I'm not here for the retreat," the young man said. "I'm from the television station. Lionel Foille promised me a big scoop."

A guest jumped up so swiftly that his chair tipped over backward. "You are mistaken. Lionel promised my magazine, *Grandmother's Rose Garden*, an exclusive."

2

Lionel chuckled as he approached the arguing reporters, patting the Pomeranian tucked in the crook of his arm. "Now, now. My news is incredible, and there's plenty of story to go around. You'll both have to wait to hear the big announcement in a few minutes."

Watson's new friend rolled past Faith in her wheelchair, and Watson blinked up at her from the woman's lap, as if to comment on the ridiculous behavior of humans.

Faith had to agree. The retreat had not even begun, and already Lionel was at the center of two controversies.

She was so focused on the situation that she was startled when Wolfe touched her arm.

"Good morning." Wolfe kissed her cheek lightly.

Faith couldn't keep from smiling, despite the drama unfolding in the garden. Her heart always beat a little faster when her fiancé was near. Wearing a designer suit and tie, he was clearly the best-dressed man in the garden. And in Faith's decidedly biased opinion, he was also the most handsome.

Marlene rushed over to Lionel once again, raising her voice to be heard above the quarreling reporters. "Let's discuss this calmly."

"What's going on?" Wolfe asked Faith.

"Lionel Foille seems to have a way of stirring people up. He promised two different reporters exclusive interviews. Marlene is trying to keep the peace, which I think we all expected to be easier with a group of gardeners."

"It appears she could use some help," Wolfe observed, leading Faith over to the group.

"Is everything all right?" Wolfe asked Marlene.

The assistant manager seemed relieved to see her boss. "These two gentlemen have a disagreement over who has the right to break Mr. Foille's announcement first."

Lionel and the others turned to Wolfe.

"First of all, welcome to the manor. I'm Wolfe Jaxon, the co-owner. Everyone has been looking forward to this retreat, and I'm sure we all want to see it run as smoothly as possible. Now please tell me what the issue is."

The reporters each explained the correspondence they'd had with Lionel. Faith thought both had reason to believe he would be breaking an exclusive news story about the TV personality.

Fortunately, Wolfe had a solution. "Perhaps Mr. Foille could grant the reporter from the magazine an interview with exclusive details, since they publish every month. The television reporter could have the scoop by breaking today's announcement on the evening news."

This seemed to appease the two reporters, and Lionel heartily agreed.

Marlene released an audible sigh of relief. "Now I can return my attention to preparing for the opening of the event." She scurried away.

Wolfe reached for Faith's hand and gave it a gentle squeeze. "Do you have a few minutes?"

"I'm afraid Marlene is going to need all the help she can get." As the manor librarian and archivist, Faith was still an employee. Although she would soon be married to Wolfe, she took her job seriously.

"Marlene has everything under control," Wolfe said. "I won't keep you long."

Faith strolled with Wolfe out of the garden and along a flagstone path. Whimsical hand-lettered signs declaring *This Way to the Wonders of Compost*, *From Garbage to Table*, and *Waste Not, Want Not* guided them and several guests to the gardening shed.

"I'm surprised to see you here," Faith said. "I thought you were attending meetings in Boston all day."

"My early conference call was canceled, so I came to see the biogas generator demo," he explained. "Eban suggested we purchase one for the manor to recycle the excess grass clippings. The lawns produce more than the gardeners can compost."

Eban Matthews was one of the gardeners who tended the manor's expansive grounds.

Nothing about Castleton Manor was done on a small scale. Even the gardening shed was designed with typical flair, blending in with the elegant manor. The generously sized building housed a high-tech office in addition to lawn mowers, tillers, various tools, and organic fertilizers. It was hardly a shed, but it had retained the original name from a time when gardeners used hand tools and horse-drawn equipment.

Organic farming expert Hannah Windmere had been scheduled to give a brief demonstration of a biogas generator. She owned an organic farm not far away, so she hadn't booked a suite at the manor.

Hannah greeted the arriving guests with a lazy smile. Frizzy red hair tumbled past the shoulders of her tie-dyed tunic, and her cutoffs were faded.

Faith was accustomed to seeing guests and speakers dressed more formally in keeping with the tone of the manor. Apparently, organic farmers were much more casual.

Although Hannah seemed mellow to the point of drowsy, she got right to the point and stayed on topic. "The generator converts barnyard, garden, and yard waste into methane gas." She shoveled green lawn clippings and chicken manure into a hopper, then pointed to a dome made of thick black rubber. "The waste decomposes in there, forming the gas."

"Where does the gas go?" someone asked.

"It's captured in this tank," Hannah replied, tapping a fifty-gallon blue plastic barrel. "Tubing comes from the tank to this solar-powered compressor. From there it can be used for whatever equipment you need to fuel. A barbecue grill, a patio heater, or even to provide light and heat for your home." She turned the knob on a small outdoor grill.

When a flame ignited under the grill, the small audience gasped and murmured their approval.

"I have a lot more to tell you about this process, so make sure you come to my talk this week for details on biogas conversion," Hannah said. "I'm on the schedule."

"Is that what Dr. Foille is announcing this morning?" asked a tall woman who held the leash of a bichon frise whose fur matched the color and texture of her puffy, snow-white curls. The puppy sniffed around the base of the rubber dome. "Is he going to market your biogas generators?"

"Maybe he'll sell his own," a shaggy-haired guest suggested. "Lionel has a whole line of gardening products." The young man wore beige cargo shorts and sandals. Printed on his gray T-shirt were the words *Garden in the Woods* and its blog address. A plump bird smaller than a robin perched on his shoulder, its white breast vertically striped with dark-brown feathers and its round brown body flecked with white spots.

"Lionel isn't interested in biogas." Hannah patted the generator. "Just hot air. He's a big windbag on the topic of sustainable gardening."

"Oh my." The first guest picked up her puppy and edged away. "I'm a fan of Lionel's television program. I don't think I want to hear this."

The bird on the young man's shoulder ruffled its brown feathers and blinked large orange eyes. As it rotated its head, Faith was startled to realize the small bird was an owl.

"Hey, you're upsetting Sage," the young man said. "A gardening retreat is no place for bad vibes."

Here we go again, Faith thought. Rather than allowing the situation to escalate, she jumped in. "The breakfast buffet should be open by now." She checked her watch. "In ten minutes, the retreat will officially begin. Why don't we head back so you have time for breakfast? You don't want to miss out on the food."

Guests instantly filed around the gardening shed, some expressing eagerness for their first meal from the famed Castleton Manor kitchen.

In a few moments, only Faith, Wolfe, and Hannah remained. Hannah's face flushed. "I apologize. That was totally not in keeping with my philosophy of peaceful coexistence. But when I heard the reporters arguing with Lionel earlier, it triggered me."

"Have you talked to Lionel about marketing your biogas generator?" Faith asked. "He might be interested."

"You need to understand." Hannah leaned back against the blue barrel. "When he was hired to restore a Victorian flower garden next door to my organic farm, Lionel promised he wouldn't spray pesticides. But he did, and I lost my organic certification for two years. I nearly lost my farm." Her posture was relaxed, and she spoke with complete calm, considering the severity of her accusation.

"I'm so sorry," Faith said. "You seem quite successful now."

Hannah tossed her wild red curls. "No thanks to Lionel."

"If Lionel isn't interested in alternative energy, you won't have competition for your generator," Wolfe pointed out. "That's good news for your business. Would a device this size produce enough gas to operate our outdoor grills?"

Hannah straightened. "Considering the acres of lawn and garden you'd be working with, I'd recommend building a biogas plant."

"Would we need building permits?" Wolfe asked.

He was probably imagining, as Faith was, an operation the size of a small utility company.

"A biogas plant doesn't take up much more room than your current composting area," Hannah answered. "The difference is that the decomposition chamber is mostly underground."

"Is there a danger of explosion?" Wolfe pointed at the red-and-black warning labels on the side of the biogas generator: *Flammable Methane* and *Explosive Hazard*.

"Hardly," Hannah said. "But government regulations require the labels. The risk of a biogas generator exploding is miniscule."

Faith motioned to another red-and-black caution sticker on the generator's dome warning of asphyxiation, with a cartoon-style figure inhaling a puffy cloud into its lungs. "What about this?"

"Regulations." Hannah waved a dismissive hand at the generator. "The greatest danger is having your sense of smell offended when you open the hopper to load materials. But like a well-maintained compost pile, the smell's not overwhelming."

Marlene's voice came over the speakers. "Good morning, and welcome to Castleton Manor. Please take your seats."

"Thank you for the information," Wolfe said to Hannah. "I have more questions, but I need to head to work." He escorted Faith along the flagstone path and back to the tables arranged on the neatly trimmed grass.

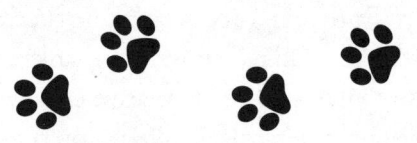

At first, the cat felt disconcerted as he sat in the wheeled lady's lap. She was sitting still, but the chair rolled over the garden paths and green grass more smoothly than a human walking. He settled in, content with the woman's murmured conversation and constant gentle pats.

"Do you like salmon, kitty?"

They had not yet been formally introduced, so the cat forgave her for calling him by an incorrect name. Besides, "kitty" was better than his human's nickname for him. "Rumpy" was a completely undignified descriptor for his bobbed tail.

He accepted the human's offering of a delightful piece of salmon. As he groomed his face afterward, he noticed his person chatting with the nice man. In the cat's opinion, she spent too much time with him these days, neglecting her clearly more important duties to her feline companion.

He supposed he could hop down and join his human, but the lady with the wheels gave him the amount of attention and salmon that he deserved.

As they rolled past the dog that resembled a fox, who was restrained by a leash, the cat cast him a smug look.

Faith approached an empty table toward the back of the seating area.

Wolfe held a chair for her, then leaned close to whisper, "I'll see you this evening."

Faith smiled at him and then faced the podium, where Marlene stood. The assistant manager appeared to be in control again, with not a single hair out of place despite the earlier difficulties.

The majority of the guests already occupied the cloth-covered round tables surrounded by flower beds. Others were still loading their plates with delicious brunch dishes. The savory aroma of eggs, sausage, and coffee competed with the scent of summer flowers.

Faith scanned the area for her parents, but they were not in the crowd. Watson was missing too. She finally saw him still perched on the lap of the lady in the wheelchair. She briefly considered retrieving him so he could sit on her lap, but he appeared content, and the woman seemed delighted. The woman was obviously an animal lover, and Faith wondered why she hadn't brought her own pet.

When people were settled, Marlene introduced retreat director Rose Fairwell. An Extension Master Gardener with a degree in horticulture, Rose was well qualified to guide the retreat. Marlene beckoned to Rose, then took her seat.

The audience clapped as the director approached the podium.

"The Hidden Treasures Literary and Gardening Retreat was inspired by *The Secret Garden*," Rose began. "The beloved children's novel was written in 1911 by Frances Hodgson Burnett, only sixteen years after Castleton Manor was built."

A few of the guests turned to admire the spectacular mansion.

Rose lifted a canvas tote bag in a bright floral print. "Everything you need is in the bag you received at registration, including the retreat schedule and a map of the manor and its grounds."

Some of the guests opened their bags and perused the contents.

"Many events will take place outdoors," Rose continued, "so we have included a refillable water bottle and a tube of sunscreen. Be sure to reapply sunscreen often while you enjoy the manor's extensive grounds. Please note that the maze can be difficult to navigate for the casual explorer. Staff will be watching out for us, but if you do become lost, you can call the front desk for help. I suggest everyone enter the number into your phones right now. You can find it on the first page of the schedule."

There was a flurry of movement as the guests pulled out their cell phones and tapped the number into their contacts.

"That's all the business we need to address." Rose smiled. "Now for the fun stuff. On each day of the retreat, a prize will be hidden in the manor or on the grounds. In keeping with our theme, fiction and nonfiction books about gardening have been creatively packaged with unique gardening supplies."

Several guests gasped in delight.

"Clues are based on *The Secret Garden*," Rose explained. "And they will be announced each morning at breakfast. I'll give you the first clue after Lionel Foille's presentation. But first, Eban Matthews will describe the fascinating history of the manor's beautiful victory garden, as he is an aspiring author as well as a first-class gardener."

Rose gestured to Eban, and he stepped up to the podium. The handsome young gardener held the audience spellbound as he discussed the manor's contributions during World War II. The manor had grown a victory garden to provide food to the citizens of the nearby village of Lighthouse Bay.

Faith had heard the story of the English-style garden many times, and soon her mind started wandering to recent events. Life would be different when she was Wolfe's wife. She felt a pang of nostalgia as she remembered her first days at the manor. She hoped her awe of the magnificent building would never fade.

Of course, there were some things she would rather forget. Dealing with difficult guests, for one. Some manor events had been challenging. Even life-threatening.

Hopefully, the rest of the gardening retreat would go smoothly. She had already witnessed Lois, Hannah, and two reporters blow up over offenses allegedly committed by Lionel.

Surely the worst was over.

3

As the history talk drew to a close, Faith's parents entered the garden. They chatted with Brooke while they filled their plates from the buffet table, which reminded Faith that she needed to have brunch too. She waved at her parents, then motioned to the seats she had saved for them.

Faith made her way to the food table, passing guests who pored over retreat schedules as they sipped tea or coffee. After gathering delectable tidbits from Brooke, including a mini quiche and fresh fruit, she met her parents at the table.

Dad held the back of a chair for Mom, then gently pushed in her seat. He gave her a quick kiss on the cheek before taking the chair beside her.

How cute. I hope Wolfe and I are still so much in love after four decades of marriage. "All settled?" Faith asked.

"We're refreshed and ready for adventure," her father declared.

"That's good to hear," Faith said. With any luck, the most adventure they would have was learning about new gardening techniques or meeting a favorite author.

"What did we miss?" her mother asked.

Just a dog that resembles a fox, fighting guests, and dueling reporters. But Faith decided to leave those parts out. "Rose Fairwell formally opened the retreat. She reminded everyone to drink plenty of water and use sunscreen. Then Eban Matthews, a staff gardener, read from his history of the manor's victory garden."

"Oh, I would have liked to hear that," her mother said.

"His book is for sale in the manor gift shop," Faith said. "It's a slim volume but packed with information. And Charlotte will be able to tell you even more. By the way, she has arranged several get-togethers with you and Dad during the retreat."

Her mom smiled. "Wonderful. I'm looking forward to getting to know Wolfe's mother better. And I can't wait to see Eileen tomorrow."

Eileen Piper was Mom's younger sister, the head librarian at the Candle House Library in Lighthouse Bay, and the leader of the Candle House Book Club. Faith, Brooke, and their friend Midge Foster rounded out the group.

Rose took the podium again. "Lionel Foille hardly needs an introduction to this audience."

The crowd responded with lighthearted chuckles and nods of agreement.

"I'm glad we didn't miss Lionel," her dad said.

Rose continued with Lionel's impressive résumé, which included restoring Victorian-era herb and flower gardens on East Coast estates, his numerous best-selling gardening how-to books, and his long television career, beginning with a public television program and leading to his popular show on a home and gardening channel.

When Rose finished, Lionel handed his Pomeranian to a petite brunette seated at his table, then walked to the podium. "Linda Bowman is my invaluable personal assistant," he said. "She watches my puppy, Patches, with as much care as if he were her own. I'm sure this audience can appreciate what an invaluable service she provides."

The members of the audience with their hands free applauded. The rest held animal companions in their arms.

Lionel spoke for thirty minutes about the history of roses. Faith's parents were silent, soaking up every word.

But Faith noticed that not everyone was attentive. Hannah stared at a flower bed, a bored expression on her face. Lois carried on a conversation with two fans, despite the glares shot her way by annoyed guests at a nearby table.

"So you can understand why the rose became a symbol of love,"

Lionel concluded. He motioned to a handsome African American man who sat at the table next to Linda.

The man picked up a rose in a clay pot from the center of the table, then walked over to the podium. Lionel wasn't short, but the man towered over him.

"That's one tall fellow," Faith's father whispered. "He's well over six feet."

"Please allow me to introduce you to my apprentice, Damian Winston," Lionel said, motioning to the man standing next to him. "In addition to all the wonderful work Damian helps me with, he has successfully implemented urban gardening programs in inner-city neighborhoods."

The crowd clapped.

"I can't begin to tell you how gratifying it is to see so many fans gathered on this beautiful summer day," Lionel said. "It is quite fitting that you should be the first ones to hear the wonderful news I have to share."

Damian handed Lionel the flowerpot.

"I am thrilled to say that I have discovered a rare rose variety," Lionel announced.

An odd look crossed Damian's face, but he quickly recovered his composure.

"I present to you a variety of climbing rose that was believed to be lost." Lionel smiled as he held up the pot. Dozens of delicate pink flowers dotted vines lush with small green leaves that clung to a post in the center of the pot.

"Those would be perfect for the trellis by our garden gate," her father said.

There was no need to whisper, as the audience was clapping enthusiastically. Some of the guests even gave a standing ovation.

Lionel gave the pot back to Damian, then gestured for people to take their seats.

Once everyone was settled, Lionel spoke at length about how he had discovered the rose at an estate sale, the site of a garden restoration project. He said the owner had not understood the significance of an old packet of seeds and dried-up bits of root.

"The young man standing next to Lionel looks like he has a case of sour stomach," her mother whispered.

Indeed, Damian wore an expression somewhere between pain and disgust.

An elderly audience member stood. She waved one hand while gripping the handle of a cane with the other. "What do you plan to name the new rose?"

Rather than being disturbed by the outburst, Lionel wore a smug smile. He again took the potted rose from Damian and held it up.

The audience was silent, and the hands of the two reporters hovered over their tablets.

Lionel rattled off a scientific name that began with *Rosa*. "I give you the Hortense Danford climbing rose, named after the estate where the seeds were discovered."

Damian jerked as though he'd been slapped. He turned and fled the garden.

Linda clutched the Pomeranian tightly as she watched Damian leave, but no one else seemed to pay attention to his abrupt departure. Instead, the crowd erupted into applause once more.

Lionel seemed to leave a trail of angry people wherever he went, but the enraptured audience hung on his every word. Even her parents seemed smitten with the bombastic man as he touted his accomplishments and his amazing discovery.

"Please join us tonight at the banquet," Lionel said. "I will discuss how it is just as important to preserve heirloom flowers as it is to preserve heirloom vegetables."

After basking in enthusiastic applause, Lionel strolled back to his seat and took Patches from Linda.

Rose returned to the podium. "Our guest authors are available to sign books before the first sessions of the retreat begin. The manor gift shop is fully stocked with their newest volumes, so make sure you get your signed copies."

Several guests got up and started to gather their tote bags and pets.

"Before you go," Rose said, "I have the first clue to finding a wonderful prize. This is an easy one for any fan of *The Secret Garden*. What type of bird does orphan Mary Lennox befriend in her uncle's garden?" She stepped away from the podium.

Several guests turned to their companions and appeared to discuss the clue.

Lionel might have angered some people, but many of his fans flocked to his table to have their gardening books autographed. Faith's parents lined up with the rest. Linda directed traffic, keeping fans in an orderly line and allowing only brief interactions with the famous gardener.

Faith was glad to see that Lois also had a line of fans, although not as long as Lionel's. Perhaps enjoying the attention of her readers would soothe Lois's anger. As the guests waited in her line, most of them petted Reynard. The dog could barely contain his excitement at being adored by dozens of people.

It was time for her to get to work. Faith scanned the garden for Watson, certain that he would be ready to join her in one of his favorite places, the opulent library.

She spotted Watson still sitting on his new friend's lap as she buzzed around the garden in her motorized wheelchair. The woman joined the line of fans at Lois's table.

Faith felt a pang of jealousy and chided herself for such a ridiculous notion.

But the ugly feeling still churned in her stomach as she told her parents where she would be and headed for the manor.

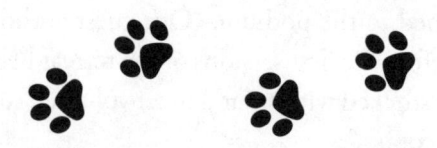

After the human made an announcement, the wheeled lady became excited and started chattering about robins.

In an effort to show his appreciation for the lady's kind attention, the cat decided to take her where the birds lived. The humans had affixed platforms under the eaves of the gardening shed, where the birds built their nests. If the humans had intended to lure the birds for the benefit of hungry cats, they had failed miserably. The wooden platforms were out of reach.

The cat hopped off the lady's lap. He trotted toward the place of birds, then glanced over his shoulder.

"Where are you going, kitty?"

He took a few more steps, then waited for the lady to catch up.

Her wheeled chair whirred on the flagstone path toward the gardening shed. She paused, seeming uncertain.

The cat trotted back to her, mewed, then continued along the path.

"You want me to follow you?"

He mewed again.

The lady followed. When she saw the bird-nesting platforms, she clapped in delight. "What a smart kitty! You knew I was searching for robins, the clue to finding the first prize."

He hopped back onto her lap and purred as she rubbed his head.

She stopped suddenly. "What is that?" She pointed to a bit of ribbon protruding from a planter bursting with flowers.

The cat liked ribbons. He leaped from her lap directly into the planter.

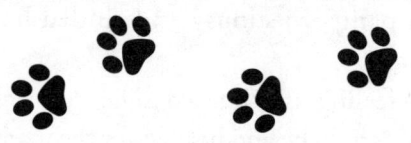

Just as Faith reached the manor door, she heard a commotion on the far side of the garden. *Not another disagreement already.*

But no, these were happy sounds on the warm summer air. Faith watched the woman in the wheelchair roll gracefully across the lawn, with both Watson and a brightly wrapped parcel in her lap.

Rose smiled. "Congratulations, Ms. Driftwood."

"Please call me Betsy. This amazing kitty led me right to the prize." Betsy ran a hand along Watson's back, smoothing his impeccably groomed fur. "I wouldn't have found the robins or the package in the flower planter without his help."

Is that a smile on Watson's face? Faith suspected her cat of tipping the odds in Betsy's favor.

"What did you discover?" the white-haired guest with the bichon frise asked.

"Let's find out." Betsy tugged at the ribbon.

Watson lent a paw by helping to remove the ribbon.

Betsy squealed when she opened the box. "It's a complete set of Lois Girten's gardening mystery series. And a gardening smock, with pink-handled gardening tools in the pockets."

"Oh, I'm so envious," the white-haired guest said. "I love Lois's series, and that smock is darling."

"I can't wait to read the books, and I can certainly use the tools," Betsy responded. "I have raised beds on stilts, and I do all my gardening from my chair. I'm determined not to let anything keep me from doing what I love."

"Is that your adorable kitty?" the woman asked.

"I'm afraid not," Betsy said. "He adopted me after I arrived."

Faith opened her mouth in surprise. Watson was not available for adoption, no matter what he thought. She began to step forward to claim her cat, then paused. Watson could sense when someone needed his comfort, so maybe Betsy could use his companionship right now. Still, Betsy needed to understand that Watson was not some stray.

"Congratulations on finding the prize." Faith extended a hand, which Betsy grasped in a solid handshake. "I'm Faith Newberry, the librarian here at the manor. And your new friend is my cat, Watson."

"Nice to meet you," Betsy said. "I hope you don't mind that your dear Mr. Watson has been showing me around the garden."

Watson looked up at Faith, blinking once slowly. That was his typical signal that he was in agreement. But with what? Was he trying to tell Faith he intended to accompany Betsy during her stay?

"Watson knows the manor inside and out," Faith said. "His favorite place is our beautiful library. I'm going there now."

Watson stretched, and for a moment Faith thought he was going to come with her. But then he resettled himself on Betsy's lap. Obviously, he had no intention of joining Faith at work at the moment.

She wanted to be annoyed, but Betsy seemed like such a pleasant person. She excused herself and headed to the library, expecting Watson to follow. He didn't.

Faith opened the library to guests eager to enjoy a mystery novel or a gardening book in the plush, velvet-upholstered chairs in front of the ornately carved fireplace. She'd put together a special display for the retreat, and the guests who visited the library perused the books she'd chosen. Instead of containing burning logs, the massive fireplace was decorated with fresh bouquets of flowers grown in the gardens.

The library maintained a tranquil, pleasantly flower-scented calm for the rest of the day. There was no sign of Watson.

At the end of the day, Faith locked up the library and hurried to her home behind the Victorian garden. The stone exterior of the gardener's cottage appeared sturdy enough to weather any storm. Modern renovations made for a bright and cheerful interior. She opened the front door, hoping to be greeted by her cat.

Instead, her father sat in the comfortable chair that Faith usually shared with Watson. He glanced up from the newspaper in his lap and smiled. "How was work?"

"It was wonderful as always," Faith said. "But the retreat is another issue."

He cocked his head. "How so?"

Faith sat down on the sofa. "I need your opinion. Your experience as a police sergeant honed your instincts for detecting trouble."

"There might have been as much self-preservation as instinct involved," her dad said. "What's bothering you?"

"Lionel seems to attract controversy." Faith told him about Lois's angry complaint, the reporters fighting for an exclusive interview, and Hannah's serious accusation. "And you saw how Damian fled the garden." She sighed. "I might be in for a stressful time."

"You'll do fine." His fatherly reassurance seemed automatic. "I didn't witness the other incidents, but I did notice Damian's reaction. From the expression on his face, I thought perhaps the rose smelled bad. So when your mother reached Lionel's table to have her book autographed, I took the opportunity to smell the rose, but there was nothing unusual about the scent."

Faith wondered why Damian had reacted that way. Did he have an issue with Lionel too?

4

Faith laughed. "Even after retiring from the police department, you're still sniffing for clues."

Her dad grinned. "You come by it honestly."

Faith took a seat on the couch. "Where's Mom?"

"She's dressing for the banquet tonight." Her father returned his attention to the newspaper. "I think she's concerned about appearing suitably fashionable for the Jaxons. It seems to me they should count themselves lucky that Wolfe found a Newberry willing to marry into their family."

Local legend had said that Faith's ancestor Josiah Newberry had been cheated out of his riches and murdered by Wolfe's ancestor Angus Jaxon in the 1800s. Even though Faith had learned the truth and shared it with her father, he still seemed to be struggling with the idea. Faith wondered if anything could completely dispel her father's certainty that the Jaxons had somehow wronged the Newberrys. And now she was marrying into the family.

"Besides, your mother is very beautiful," he continued. "Her style and grace put any woman to shame."

"What's that?" Her mom entered the room, fiddling with an earring. She had changed from her poppy-print sundress to a summer-weight linen dress in a subdued lavender, her hair pulled back with a clip.

Her father rose. "I was paying you a compliment." He pulled Mom into his arms and spun around Faith's small living room. "Reminding our daughter that she has a very beautiful mother."

Mom stopped and frowned at Dad's dress shirt and slacks. "Dinner is at six. Where's your tie?"

"I refuse to wear one." His tone was breezy, but there was a stubborn undertone. "This is supposed to be a retreat. A vacation. When I retired, I vowed to never wear a tie again. Well, except for Faith's wedding."

"But as a police sergeant, you didn't wear a tie every day," her mother reminded him.

"I worked hard for the right to go casual." Dad hummed a few notes of the tune playing in his head and waltzed Mom around the living room again. "This is only dinner."

"It's a banquet, so most men will be wearing ties." Her mother smiled at Faith. "It was hard to convince your father to wear a tuxedo for his own wedding."

"Our wedding. Neighborhood church. Family and friends. Reception in the church social hall. Nice and simple."

As children, Faith and her sister, Jenna, had spent many hours studying their parents' wedding album. The affair had appeared to be as elegant as a young couple starting out in life could afford. Mom's white dress had layers of lace and hundreds of faux pearls. Dad had rented a black tuxedo with a bow tie.

"It only seemed simple to you because the groom rarely has much to do with the planning," her mother said. "Believe me, it took effort to organize. That's why Jenna and I are helping Faith."

"Is it my fault that you make everything look effortless?" Dad hummed the tune a final time, then stopped and kissed Mom on the cheek. "Let's go."

Faith's father wasn't the only gentleman opting for less formal attire. Even some women seemed more prepared for a picnic than a banquet.

The young man who'd been at the biogas generator demonstration now wore blue jeans and hiking boots, with the same T-shirt advertising the *Garden in the Woods* blog. Long pants probably qualified as formal in his world, even if they were denim.

The tiny owl on his shoulder flapped one wing, drawing the attention of every cat in the room.

Faith supposed the gardening retreat attendees' attire was a sort of costume. The banquet hall had hosted many meals with guests dressed to fit a literary or historical theme. The vast space, ornately carved cornices, and ceiling soaring to arched beams reminded Faith of a medieval cathedral. On this warm August night, a small fire flickered in the enormous alabaster fireplace, more for effect than heat. Beautiful chandeliers softly illuminated the room, and stunning floral arrangements lightly scented the air.

She allowed her parents a moment to take in the stunning scene, then led them to the table where Wolfe sat with his mother, Charlotte.

Wolfe and Charlotte rose to greet Faith's parents. Wolfe held Faith's chair as she took her seat. Dad assisted Charlotte, then Mom.

A server arrived with their salads. The salad was a visual and culinary delight, prepared from locally harvested organic butter lettuce studded with slivers of fresh apricot, roasted walnuts, and edible nasturtiums.

The conversation turned to a recap of the day's events, and Charlotte and Faith's parents shared stories about the talks they had attended.

As they chatted, Faith counted her blessings to have such wonderful parents and that she would soon be part of another kind family.

As if he were thinking the same thing, Wolfe caught her eye and smiled.

The main course of braised lamb, with equally delicious side dishes of Hasselback potatoes and green beans with caramelized shallots, drew compliments from the guests. The only thing that could have made Faith's evening better was if Watson had chosen to spend time with his family instead of his new friend Betsy.

At the conclusion of the main course, thick slices of chocolate cake—topped with a dollop of fresh whipped cream and strawberries from a local farm—were served.

The buzzing of dozens of conversations stilled as Rose stepped to the podium. "Again, thank you for attending this retreat. I know we all enjoyed the opening sessions earlier today and this marvelous dinner." She smiled. "I'm pleased to announce that Betsy Driftwood is the lucky person to find the first day's hidden treasure."

The audience cheered for Betsy.

"Tonight's speaker hardly needs an introduction," Rose said, then gave a brief biography of Lionel Foille.

Instinctively, Faith glanced around the room, but she didn't see Lionel.

Rose stopped as Damian approached the podium and touched her sleeve. She smiled as he whispered to her. The smile froze, then melted in alarm.

Guests murmured and shifted in their chairs, scanning the banquet hall. They were verifying what Faith had already observed: Lionel was not in the room.

Rose hurried to where Marlene was seated.

Faith had seen Marlene deal with many last-minute schedule changes during events, and she'd rarely witnessed Marlene lose her composure. Guests might not notice, but Faith could tell by the twitch at the corner of her mouth that Marlene had been caught unprepared.

The young man with the shaggy hair and the tiny owl on his shoulder removed the linen napkin from his lap, stood, and walked over to the two women.

While the trio had a brief whispered conversation, the owl observed the crowd from his perch.

Rose returned to the podium. "Ladies and gentlemen, there has been an unexpected change in the schedule."

The grumbling stopped, replaced by speculative murmurs.

"Unfortunately, Lionel Foille is unavailable to give his talk tonight,"

Rose went on. "But we have an equally interesting substitution. While gardening is an ancient art, Jeremiah Fielding blends his avid use of social media with an off-grid lifestyle. His blog *Garden in the Woods* has thousands of fans eager to learn how to use solar energy and modern greenhouse materials to maintain a subsistence life. He has generously offered to speak on the topic of soil enrichment in a poor soil environment."

The audience clapped politely.

"After Jeremiah's discussion, we will adjourn to the loggia as scheduled," Rose said. "The Lighthouse Bay High School will give us a preview of their Wednesday evening performance of *The Secret Garden*." She nodded to Jeremiah and left the podium.

Jeremiah took her place. "Before I begin, please allow me to introduce my friend Sage, who is a northern pygmy owl."

The owl hooted softly.

"His wing was damaged beyond repair when he tangled with a Maine coon cat. He can't return to the wild, so I was allowed to adopt him." Jeremiah grinned. "Now, let's talk about dirt."

Faith couldn't imagine finding soil interesting, but Jeremiah was a skilled speaker. She guessed Lionel would be upset that his replacement had enthralled the audience with such a seemingly mundane topic. She was so enraptured that she nearly forgot to wonder what could possibly keep Lionel away from a packed audience of eager fans.

Nearly.

Jeremiah concluded his impromptu speech to hearty laughter and applause.

Rose returned to the podium and directed the guests to the loggia for the play preview.

Wolfe excused himself, due to an early meeting in Boston tomorrow morning.

Faith's mother chatted with Charlotte as they walked to the loggia.

Her father offered his arm to Faith. "Are you aware your mother is planning the wedding of the century?"

Faith nodded. "Do you remember all the fuss over Jenna's wedding?"

"True. However, your sister's wedding plans paled in comparison to what your mother and Charlotte are putting together." He paused, pulling Faith to a halt. "I'm sorry, honey. Maybe that's what you want. A wedding fit for a princess."

Faith shrugged. "I already feel like I'm living a fairy tale, marrying my Prince Charming. I don't need a big wedding, but the Jaxons have many business and social connections who expect to be invited."

"I understand," her father said. "I'm only concerned the wedding is going to cost more than the annual budget of some small countries."

Faith hoped he didn't expect to be held to the tradition of the father of the bride footing the entire bill. But she knew that he did believe in tradition. Now was definitely not the right time to ask him about it, though.

They walked through the French doors and onto the loggia. Padded folding chairs were arranged in rows under the covered patio facing one of the manor's many gorgeous gardens. A stage had been erected in the midst of lush beds bursting with blooms. The warm summer breeze swayed the strings of sparkling white lights under the loggia roof.

"Let's sit here," Charlotte said, leading the way. "We'll have a nice view of the stage."

Faith noticed Watson still seated on Betsy's lap in a front-row aisle seat. He hadn't dropped by the library once the entire day, apparently choosing to travel around the retreat events on his new friend's lap. Even though Faith was surrounded by her parents and her soon-to-be mother-in-law, she couldn't help but feel a bit abandoned.

After the guests filled the seats, Marlene stepped onto the stage to announce the sneak preview of Wednesday night's play based on *The Secret Garden*.

Before she finished speaking, Patches dashed up the wooden steps, stopped in front of Marlene, and began to bark.

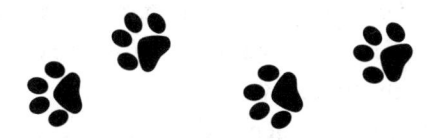

The cat did not speak dog well, but he knew enough to recognize distress in the small dog's yips. The human onstage tried to hush the dog, and the rest of the humans chuckled. But this was no laughing matter.

A few seats away, the annoying dog that resembled a fox jerked the leash away from his person. The dog's human shouted in alarm, but the cat could tell the larger dog intended no harm. He wanted to help the small dog.

As the manor's four-legged representative, the cat felt obligated to assist. He hopped down from his perch on his new friend's lap.

The little dog danced around the ankles of the woman onstage. Some humans roared with laughter, but others yelled with alarm when the other dog raced onto the stage and the little dog bolted for the far steps.

The cat had no choice but to follow.

Faith hurried down the loggia steps when Watson joined the chase. She didn't want him in trouble with Marlene again. Even though Faith was the fiancée of the manor's co-owner, she knew Marlene wouldn't bend the rules for her cat.

While the audience seemed entertained, the assistant manager was obviously angry. "Ms. Girten, your dog," Marlene sputtered. "Where is Mr. Foille? Faith, stop that cat!"

Lionel's assistant, Linda, ran onto the stage just as the animals disappeared down the far steps.

Lois bypassed the stage, running around the front in an attempt to cut them off at the base of the steps.

Faith followed close on Lois's heels. It may have appeared comical to the audience, but Faith was concerned the Pomeranian might be a bite-size snack for the Shiba Inu.

Several high school students, dressed in period costumes from the 1910s, followed.

The little dog ran through the maze of garden beds and along the flagstone path leading to the gardening shed. A motion sensor light flicked on as the animals and humans approached the building. The large garage-style doors were closed.

Patches ran past a pile of freshly mowed grass to Hannah's biogas generator. A large man was slumped over the hopper opening.

As Faith neared the generator, she noticed in the dim light a smear of something dark partially hidden by the ring of salt-and-pepper hair circling his scalp.

"Lionel!" Linda called. "What are you doing?"

"He appears to be unconscious." Lois grabbed her dog's leash. "How horrible! Has he been here all afternoon?"

"No." Linda shook Lionel's shoulder. "He was resting in his room until two, preparing for his speech tonight." She tugged on the man's arm. "Lionel, wake up!"

Patches circled his ankles, whining and nipping at the hems of his slacks.

Linda pulled Lionel's face away from the hopper opening.

He slumped to the ground, a blank expression in his open eyes.

5

Linda's screams rang in her ears as Faith leaped into the steps she had learned in CPR class. The first and most important was directing someone to call emergency services. "Call 911," she instructed Lois.

The author pulled a cell phone from her pocket and punched in the numbers.

Faith returned her attention to Lionel. She spotted some kind of mark on his head. She couldn't see it very well in the shed's security light, but it might have been a smear of dirt or maybe even blood. She had an uneasy feeling he was beyond assistance.

When the paramedics arrived, Faith stepped away from Lionel and joined Marlene and Rose.

The crowd behind the gardening shed had grown. Curious and concerned guests speculated about what had happened to the famous gardener.

Betsy rolled her wheelchair close to Faith. "That cute little dog knew his master was in trouble. What a good boy."

Watson had apparently concluded his mission. He hopped onto Betsy's lap. Faith could hear him purring as the woman stroked his black-and-white fur.

Lighthouse Bay Police Chief Andy Garris arrived and immediately took control of the tense scene. "Please move the guests out of this area. My officers need full, unimpeded access."

Marlene herded the onlookers away from the gardening shed. "Everyone, please return to your seats on the loggia."

Faith lingered, thinking the chief might want a statement since she was one of the people who had discovered Lionel. As she peered over to see how the gardener was doing, she saw one of the paramedics glance up at Chief Garris and shake his head. Faith shivered. As she'd suspected, Lionel Foille was gone.

"There's nothing you can do here," Jan Rooney said, breaking into Faith's thoughts. The petite officer wore a short-sleeved uniform shirt in deference to the summer heat, exposing deeply tanned olive skin. "I suggest you join the others. Go watch the play."

"It's only a sneak preview," Faith said. "I'll see the entire play Wednesday night. Did you see the mark on Lionel's head? I didn't get a good look at it, but it might have been a smear of dirt or blood."

"Don't you have enough to keep you busy?" Rooney folded her arms across her chest. "Like planning your wedding?"

"Well, yes. But shouldn't you take my statement while the incident is still fresh in my mind?"

The officer narrowed her eyes. "We'll be interviewing everyone later, but I suppose you were one of the first on the scene. As usual." She pulled out a tablet and tapped it a few times. "All right, you know the routine."

Faith relayed what she had observed, including Marlene's introduction of the play preview, Lionel's Pomeranian running onstage, the Shiba Inu and Watson chasing the little dog back to the gardening shed, and finally the horrible discovery of Lionel draped over the biogas generator. "Maybe he was struck with something and fell over the hopper opening."

"From the warning labels plastered all over the machine, I would think simply poking his head in that opening would be enough to asphyxiate him."

"Lionel couldn't have missed those warnings," Faith said. "The lights on the shed are motion activated, so they would have been on. He would have known not to inhale the gas. And besides that, it stinks. I don't think a conscious person could stand to keep his head in the hopper for more than a few seconds."

"True." Officer Rooney wrinkled her nose. "Between the compost pile and this thing, I can't imagine why anyone would want to hang around back here."

"You'd be surprised," Faith said drily. "This retreat is populated with people who think dirt is the most wonderful thing ever. They probably wouldn't be bothered much by rotting lawn clippings." She paused as the reality of his death hit her. "Lionel was the most famous gardener here. People will be devastated. Marlene and the retreat organizers are going to have a hard time filling the gap he'll leave."

"We'll find out what happened," Rooney said, her voice softer. "Don't go poking your nose into this. More than likely, Mr. Foille expired from natural causes and just happened to be near the biogas generator at the time."

Faith hoped that turned out to be the case, but Lionel certainly had enough enemies to make his unexpected death suspicious.

Leaving the police to their work, she went back to the loggia and settled quietly into a seat next to her mother.

"I'm so glad you returned," her mother whispered. "I practically had to sit on your father to keep him from getting involved. He's supposed to be retired and on vacation, but you know how he is."

"Don't worry," Faith whispered back. "Chief Garris is territorial. He wouldn't let a retired police officer from out of town intrude on his investigation."

"What are you girls conspiring about?" her dad asked.

Before either of them could answer, Marlene stepped onto the stage. The audience hushed immediately.

Marlene glanced to either side of the stage as if expecting another interruption, but no parade of animals materialized. "Ladies and gentlemen, thank you for your patience." She paused. "It is with deepest regret that I must inform you that Mr. Lionel Foille has passed away."

Gasps and murmurs of alarm rippled across the loggia.

"Our thoughts and prayers go out to Mr. Foille's friends and family during this difficult time," Marlene said, then gestured for Rose to take over.

"This is a devastating loss for the gardening world, and I'm as stunned as all of you," Rose said, her voice faltering. "I can't imagine the retreat continuing without Lionel, our guiding light, leading the way." She dabbed a tissue to her eyes. "But rather than cancel the rest of this event, the retreat committee believes it would honor Lionel's memory to continue as planned."

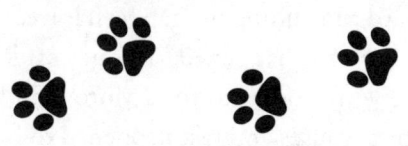

The little dog was a quivering mess of fur and distress.

The cat jumped off his new friend's lap and approached the human holding the tiny dog. The cat stood on his hind legs and tentatively placed a paw on the human's leg.

"Hello, kitty." *The human wiped tears from her cheeks with a cloth.* "What do you want?"

The cat stretched his neck, his whiskers curving toward the small dog. There was little he could do to comfort an animal who had lost his human. He could not imagine how he would cope if he were in the dog's situation. He already felt a little like he was losing his person to the nice man, but she was still alive and well, even if she was ignoring him.

"Patches, see the sweet kitty?" *the human asked.* "He wants to say hello."

The dog stopped shivering for a moment and focused on the cat.

The human knelt so the dog and cat could sniff each other.

There was so much more than a mere greeting the cat wished he could convey.

The lady with the wheels rolled near. "There you are, Watson. Is this your friend?"

The other human patted the little dog. "I might be imagining things, but it seems like this cat came over to give Patches his sympathy."

"I wouldn't be surprised," the wheeled lady said. "He's a very special cat."

"Is he yours?"

"No. I'm actually more of a dog person, although I wouldn't mind having a cat companion like this one. Lionel's puppy must be traumatized by finding him." She extended one hand, allowing the dog to sniff her fingers before she gently stroked his fur. "What's going to become of him?"

"It's too early to tell. I am—or I guess I was—Lionel's assistant. I watch Patches during conferences, but I can't keep him."

The little dog shivered again. The poor creature was heartbroken.

The cat touched his nose to the dog's and purred, giving what comfort he could.

Something would have to be done.

Tuesday morning in the manor breakfast room, Marlene once again announced the death of Lionel. Few guests had not learned the news already, even those who hadn't attended the play preview. But Faith knew Marlene did not tolerate rumors at the manor and was determined to set the facts straight. She related that there were no developments in the investigation since last night. The police were not ready to release the cause of Lionel's death.

As the guests sat in gloomy silence, Marlene returned to her seat.

The mood in the breakfast room slowly lightened a little. Faith thought it felt odd to make small talk and enjoy the sumptuous breakfast buffet with her parents so soon after a man's abrupt and suspicious demise. Obviously the other guests felt the same way.

Linda approached Faith's table, the Pomeranian cradled in her arms. "Excuse me, but Ms. Russell suggested I talk to you."

"Yes?" Faith asked. "How may I assist you?"

"I'm going home tomorrow," Linda said. "Unfortunately, I can't take Patches with me. Ms. Russell told me the kennels here are full, but you know the local veterinarian who might be able to help."

"I'll call her for you." Faith dialed her good friend Midge, who served as the concierge vet at the manor. Midge confirmed that she could keep Patches at her clinic until Lionel's family could pick him up. Faith disconnected and smiled at Linda. "Midge is happy to help. She said you can drop off Patches at her clinic anytime."

"Thank you," Linda said. "I'm so relieved. I was worried about the little guy."

After she left, Faith's mother touched her arm and leaned close. "That poor dog will need time and lots of affection to heal from this trauma."

Faith nodded. "I can't imagine how awful it must be for him. Midge will take good care of him."

She was finishing a second cup of coffee when Rose drew the group's attention by standing and tapping a knife against her water glass.

Guests turned solemn faces her way.

"We are all shocked by Lionel's unexpected passing," Rose said. "But the best way to honor his memory is by carrying on our love of gardening. While gardening, we often discover unexpected treasure. A tomato plant produces a wildly abundant crop. A rare butterfly is drawn by blooming flowers. Friendships are formed with other gardeners. This morning I am delighted to announce the clue to finding the second hidden treasure at our retreat. In *The Secret Garden*, Mary Lennox learns that Colin Craven spends his days in bed, surrounded by an item that will lead you to the next prize."

Although some guests discussed the clue, more of the chatter focused on Lionel's death. Speculation abounded. The retreat attendees seemed genuinely distressed to lose the famous man. Although he'd had his share of enemies, Lionel was hugely popular with the public. So were his television show and books and gardening products branded with his name. The man had to be worth a fortune.

"I still can't believe Lionel is gone." Mom dabbed a cloth napkin to her eyes, then reached for Dad's hand. "You've dealt with similar tragedies many times, but I'm finding it quite a shock."

He squeezed her hand. "It's never easy, even when the victim is someone you don't know."

"I almost felt as if I did know him," Mom said. "He was in our home every week with his gardening program, and it always seemed like he was talking to us as a friend. To imagine him like that . . ."

Faith took her mother's free hand, trying to comfort her. There were plenty of tears and sniffling in the breakfast room, although Faith suspected there were a few people who weren't sad that Lionel was gone.

When her mother had recovered her composure, Faith recalled something her father had said. "Dad, you called Lionel a victim. Do you suspect foul play?"

Her father raised both hands. "Force of habit. Anyway, this isn't my case. I know how I'd feel if some out-of-towner barged in on my investigation."

"If someone passes away from natural causes, there's no need for an investigation, right?" Faith asked.

"If an elderly person who has been ill dies at home or in the hospital, there probably isn't an investigation," her father answered. "Lionel was older, but he seemed hale and hearty. His passing was unexpected and in a public place. Not knowing the circumstances, the police had to secure the scene. There may be nothing suspicious about his death, but they won't know until the coroner examines him."

Her mom glanced at Faith. "I hope you're not tempted to become involved in another case."

Her parents knew about Faith getting caught up in several mysteries at the manor, but she hadn't divulged all the details. Especially the dangerous ones.

"According to Dad, there may not be a case." Faith lifted her coffee mug to her lips, then paused. "Does Lionel have any children?"

"You mean potential heirs willing to bump him off in order to inherit?" her dad asked. "I believe he has two sons, but they're partners in the business. Their father would be worth more to them alive."

"Stop it, you two," her mother scolded. "Faith, look. Your Watson is following the woman in the wheelchair."

Betsy rolled from the buffet to a cloth-covered table nearby, Watson behind her. When she was situated, Watson hopped onto her lap.

Her mother must have read the expression of dismay on Faith's face because she said, "It's perfectly natural. You're spending more time with Wolfe and planning a wedding. Watson feels left out. He's seeking companionship."

"The guests will be leaving in a few days. I suppose I need to let Watson enjoy his new friendships." Faith checked her watch. "Right now, I need to open the library."

Faith was determined to stay on schedule and uphold the manor's reputation for hosting well-planned and smoothly running events.

Even when a suspicious death threatened to throw everything into disarray.

Guests crowded the library during breaks between presentations. Many snapped photos with cameras or cell phones. One guest pressed her hand against the walnut paneling, as though testing whether it was real. She didn't know how close she was to discovering one of the many hidden passages in the manor. Another craned his neck, staring up at the second-story bookshelves on the upper level.

As Faith answered questions about everything from the number of books in the collection to whether the red fabric covering the chairs and sofas was real velvet, she was mercifully distracted from both Lionel's death and her cat's straying affections.

Jeremiah strolled in. He wore sandals that seemed sturdy enough for mountain climbing, cargo shorts, and a sky-blue T-shirt with the same logo for his blog.

As Jeremiah and the owl on his shoulder took in the vast library, Faith wondered what a man who spent most of his time in the woods thought of such opulence.

He approached the desk. "Good morning, Miss Newberry." He extended a calloused hand. "Jeremiah Fielding."

"Please call me Faith." She exchanged a firm handshake with the young man. He might appear a bit rough around the edges, but he had good manners. "I enjoyed your talk last night at dinner. How may I help you?"

"I'm not sure you can," Jeremiah said. "I've been searching for an old horticultural book for years. It's referenced in other books, but I haven't been able to find a copy."

"Let me check the computer catalog." Faith turned her attention to the monitor on her desk. "I also have access to the database for the Candle House Library in Lighthouse Bay. Do you know the author and the title?"

Jeremiah consulted a tattered filing card. "*Indigenous Farming Techniques of the Pennacook* by Henry Edmond Doddard. It was written in 1798. I'd almost given up hope that a copy exists when I heard about this collection." He waved a hand, taking in both levels of floor-to-ceiling bookshelves. "A librarian in Chicago told me my best hope might be in a private collection."

"That's true," Faith agreed. "Rare books that never found their way into a public library system can often—"

She was interrupted by a bloodcurdling scream.

6

"It came from up there." A man pointed to the second floor.

A gray-haired woman bounced up and down behind the ornate railing, shrieking.

Two men clambered up the narrow stairs.

"Are you okay?" a gentleman in khakis and a sweater vest asked.

"I found the second hidden treasure!" The woman held up a large gift bag overflowing with bright tissue paper. "As soon as I heard the clue, I knew it would be near a hanging tapestry."

From the woman's scream, Faith had expected another body. While she was happy for the guest, she wished she hadn't caused such a panic with her excitement.

The trio descended the stairs.

"What's in it?" the man in the sweater vest asked.

The woman pulled out item after item, piling them on a small oak table. "Children's picture books. A pop-up gardening book. Oh, and child-size gardening tools, an apron, and rubber boots. And packets of seeds." She beamed. "My grandchildren will be thrilled. They love playing in the dirt, and now they can start their own garden at my house."

"Well, I'm glad that wasn't anything bad," Jeremiah murmured to Faith.

"I was just thinking the same thing."

Sage, the owl, ruffled his feathers, doing a good job of looking indignant.

Jeremiah checked his watch. "I need to get ready for my panel discussion."

"I'll jot down the information about your book," Faith said. "The title doesn't ring any bells, but our collection is large. Perhaps I can locate it."

"Thanks." Jeremiah paused in the doorway to allow Officer Rooney to enter the library, then waved to Faith and disappeared.

Faith tensed. She had already given her statement to the police, and the officer rarely made social calls to the manor. "Good morning. Lovely weather we're having this morning, isn't it?"

Rooney didn't seem interested in small talk. "Have you seen Lois Girten?"

"She was in the breakfast room earlier, but I haven't seen her since," Faith said. "I've been in the library, and she hasn't come in." The author would be hard to miss, with her lively dog creating a ruckus wherever he went. Faith thumbed through a retreat schedule. "She was scheduled to give a talk in the salon. The sessions are ending now. I can take you there."

"Thanks, but I know where it is." The officer turned to leave.

As if on cue, Lois entered the library, with Reynard tugging at his leash. She exchanged greetings with a few guests. Wearing a smile instead of a scowl did wonders to improve the author's appearance. Her short hair was neatly styled, and a sleek pantsuit emphasized her trim figure.

Rooney waved Lois over to Faith's desk.

Lois arched one eyebrow in a quizzical expression as she approached.

"Ms. Girten, would you mind answering a few questions?" the officer said.

Irritation flashed in Lois's eyes. "I already spoke to the police."

"I have a few follow-up questions," Rooney said.

"Fine. But I want to attend the next session in fifteen minutes."

"Don't worry." The officer took out her tablet. "This won't take long."

Intensely curious, Faith was glad when Rooney settled in to conduct her interview at Faith's desk.

"I wish these pets could speak." The officer let Reynard sniff her hand, then scratched behind the dog's ears.

Reynard wagged his tail in appreciation.

"Your dog was one of the first on the scene, right?" Rooney asked.

"Thank goodness the Pomeranian led them to Lionel after . . ." Lois paused. Her eyes filled with tears, but her expression quickly hardened. "After whatever happened to him. Do you know what killed him yet? Was it a heart attack? Or a brain embolism?"

Faith wondered whether Lois was trying to deflect the officer from the idea that Lionel might have been murdered.

"The coroner hasn't issued a report," Rooney said. "We don't know the cause of death yet."

Faith wondered why Rooney was questioning Lois if they didn't know how Lionel had died. Was the author a murder suspect?

"Were you in a session Monday afternoon?" the officer asked.

Lois frowned. "Yes. Shrubbery pruning techniques. I don't even have shrubbery in my yard. I only went because I could use the information in a novel. You know, like someone gets stabbed with pruning shears? The talk was a total yawn fest. I snuck out early."

"When was that?" Rooney riffled through the schedule on Faith's desk.

"You tell me." Lois seemed to have a temper as short as her dog's attention span.

"The session went from one to two." The officer glanced up from the schedule and fixed her gaze on Lois. "You said you left early. Can you tell me where you went?"

Lois released an exaggerated sigh. "I drove to a shop in Lighthouse Bay to purchase some treats for Reynard."

"Happy Tails Gourmet Bakery?" Faith offered. In addition to her thriving veterinary practice, Midge owned a store in town that sold pet food and treats.

"Yes," Lois said. "I'm sure the attentive clerk can confirm we were there. Reynard makes quite an impression wherever we go."

"What time was that?" Rooney jotted on her tablet.

"I'm not in the habit of keeping precise track of every moment of my day, but I'd guess we arrived around one thirty. I browsed the store for fifteen or twenty minutes, then returned to the manor."

"Did you interact with anyone once you returned?" the officer asked.

"Do you mean, do I have an alibi?" The author's cheeks flushed. "No, I suppose not. Reynard and I arrived in the middle of sessions, and I didn't run into any fans on the way to my room. Does this mean Lionel was murdered?"

Rooney ignored her question. "What time did you arrive at the manor?"

"I was back sometime after two o'clock. Reynard and I rested in our room, and then we went to a book signing at Glynde. We were there from four to six. When we returned to the manor, it was time for the banquet."

Faith remembered Linda saying that Lionel had rested in his room until two. Glynde was a nearby village, so Lois had been at the manor between two and shortly before four. The killer had struck sometime between two and six when the banquet started.

Rooney pointed at the retreat tote bag hanging from Lois's shoulder. "Do you mind showing me what's in your bag?"

Lois gasped. "You do think I killed Lionel. I'll admit I'm not sad he's gone, but I would never do such a thing. Besides, I write murder mysteries. I know the killer rarely gets away with it."

"I understand," Rooney said, her tone reasonable. "And as an author, you also know the police have to follow up on every lead."

"Seriously? You want to see what's in here?" Lois lifted the tote and upended it, spilling the contents onto Faith's desk. A retreat schedule and freebies handed out by speakers—seed packets, pens, and bookmarks—tumbled across the polished wood.

A pair of worn leather gardening gloves plopped on top of the pile. A rust-colored stain coated the thumb and first two fingers of the right-hand glove.

Lois gaped at the gloves. "Where did those come from?"

"Do you mind if I take them?" the officer asked.

"They aren't mine," Lois said. "You can have them. Why would I bring work gloves here?"

"You mean, why would you bring gardening gloves to a gardening retreat? Yes, that does seem rather unbelievable." Rooney raised one eyebrow, then removed a plastic bag from her pocket and carefully slid the gloves inside without touching them. "I'll need the bag too, please."

Lois shoved it at the police officer. "Take it. I have nothing to hide."

Rooney tapped on her tablet, thanked Lois, and left abruptly.

Reynard whined and tugged at his leash.

"You can use my bag while the police have yours." Faith emptied her retreat tote bag into a desk drawer and helped Lois load her items into it.

"I've never been so humiliated," Lois muttered. She let Reynard drag her out of the library.

Rooney had refused to state it outright, but it was obvious this was a murder investigation. Faith couldn't get involved. She had a wedding to plan and a retreat to help run.

But it would be so easy for her, a manor employee, to learn who was where between the hours of two and six.

Unless the investigation had just ended with the discovery of the stained glove in Lois's tote.

Faith didn't have long to ponder the new developments. Her parents hurried into the library, bubbling with excitement.

"I didn't think I'd like the last session," her dad said, "but it was fascinating."

"What was it about?" Faith asked.

"A professor from a liberal arts college discussed *The Secret Garden*," her mom answered. "And a horticulturist explained how a neglected garden could continue to flourish without humans tending it."

"The garden where they held the talk was something else," her father said. "I'd love to copy it in our yard at home. On a smaller scale, of course."

"Which garden was it?" Faith asked.

"The one with the topiaries," he said. "I could have a lot of fun with a pair of shears."

"I had trouble concentrating on the lecture because the surroundings in the Victorian garden were so lovely," her mom admitted.

"The Victorian garden would make a great setting for a wedding," Faith said.

Her dad grinned. "You bet it would."

"No, it would be too informal for the wedding of a man of Wolfe's stature," her mother said.

Faith started to tell her parents that Wolfe was not pretentious. For a man coming from such wealth and prestige, he was actually quite down-to-earth.

But her mother continued before Faith could speak. "Are you ready for the luncheon?" While the men went golfing, the women were heading to a restaurant in Boston.

Faith regarded her mother's outfit. Her tea-length white dress featured a delicate rose print and a full skirt. She wore a matching hat covered in bits of lacy rose tulle and silk flowers and white low-heeled sandals. Mom was prepared to meet the queen of England if the meeting were held at a garden party. Faith wore what she normally would for work—a blouse and dress pants—but she still felt underdressed. "Maybe I should change."

"We don't have time," her mother said. "You look fine."

"I can leave as soon as Laura arrives," Faith said. She had asked Laura Kettrick to take over while she was gone. Sometimes Laura assisted Faith in the library in addition to her duties as a housekeeper.

Faith had just finished packing up her purse and laptop when Laura walked in, carrying a notebook and college textbooks. Laura was pursuing a degree in library science, and Wolfe paid for every class in which she received an A.

"It's good to see you," Mom told Laura, then asked about her classes.

Faith noticed a pensive expression had settled onto her father's face. She didn't have time to find out what troubled him because Wolfe entered the library, dressed in navy pants and a white polo shirt with narrow navy stripes.

Wolfe greeted everyone warmly. His devastating smile never failed to make Faith a little weak in the knees.

He gave Faith a brief kiss on the cheek, then smiled at her father. "Are you ready? Nick and Blake will meet us there. We have a tee time of one o'clock."

Faith's brother-in-law, Nick Lynch, had carved an afternoon out of his busy schedule as a defense attorney to spend time with Faith's future husband. Wolfe's younger brother Blake, the owner of a racetrack in southern New Hampshire, had more flexibility.

Wolfe had confided to Faith that he was excited to develop a relationship with Faith's dad. He was glad to have a father in his life again after his own father had passed away years ago. Faith hoped playing golf with the Jaxon men would help her father warm up to the family.

"Am I dressed okay?" Dad glanced down at his khakis and short-sleeved button-down. He was as tall as Wolfe, but he had a larger frame and carried a few extra pounds as a result of Mom's excellent cooking. "I'm not used to hobnobbing at country clubs. Not part of a policeman's normal routine."

"You'll fit right in," Wolfe assured him.

Her father clearly wasn't convinced, but he winked at Faith and her mom. "I'll try not to share too many war stories from my time patrolling the mean streets of Springfield."

Faith and her mother entered the Jaxon family's private quarters on the third floor of the manor. The entire top floor was tastefully decorated in keeping with the mansion's elegance but with more comfort and coziness in mind.

Faith and her sister, Jenna, squealed when they saw each other and exchanged hugs. The older generation of sisters—Faith's mom and Eileen—greeted each other with equal delight, although they skipped the squealing. Brooke, Midge, and Charlotte were already in the living room, which had a stunning view of the ocean.

Someone was missing. Watson had already claimed the Jaxon home as part of his personal territory, but he was nowhere to be seen.

Aunt Eileen studied Faith. "What's wrong?"

"I was hoping Watson would be here too."

"I saw him earlier," Charlotte said. "He was prowling around the hallway."

"Then he must be nearby. Watson?" Faith was disappointed when the tuxedo cat didn't walk into the living room, even though he normally didn't come when she called.

Her mother explained to the others how Watson was upset by the changes in Faith's life. "It's a very common situation when animal companions experience the emotional upheaval of a marriage, moving to a new home, or arrival of a new baby."

"He's adopted one of the retreat guests," Faith said. "Betsy Driftwood. He must be with her."

"The lady in the sporty wheelchair?" Brooke asked. After complaining about her boring uniform yesterday, Brooke had gone all out to express her fashionista side for this lunch. She wore a black sleeveless dress sprinkled with large white polka dots. Her matching hat was adorned with a red taffeta bow the same color as her wide belt.

Faith nodded.

"I can see why Watson would make friends with her," Brooke said. "She's really nice."

"Speaking of animals in distress, what happened to Lionel's Pomeranian?" Faith asked.

"The little cutie's depressed, of course." Midge tucked a stray strand of blonde hair back under her lacy lavender organza hat. The Southern belle style matched her subtle accent, left over from her childhood in Frog Eye, Alabama. "Linda brought him to my clinic this morning, thinking a family member would pick him up. I've left messages with his sons and his sister, but I'm still waiting to hear from them."

"If my landlady allowed pets other than fish, I'd take the poor puppy rather than see him abandoned," Brooke said. Her animal companions were two angelfish named Diva and Bling.

Jenna turned, causing the hat perched precariously on her dark hair to wobble. It consisted almost entirely of an enormous silk rose nested in tulle, matching her bright-pink dress. "Maybe his family has allergies."

"That might be the case," Midge said. "If his family can't take the dog, then we'll have to find the little guy a new home."

"I should look for Watson before we go," Faith said. She peered into the hallway. "Watson?"

"I'm sure Watson is fine," Charlotte said. "Like you said, he's probably with Ms. Driftwood. If we're going to make it to our luncheon on time, we need to leave. We can chat on the ride. You never know how the traffic will be in Boston."

The cat heard his human's voice coming from another room. He thought briefly of running to her for a quick hug and ear scratch when she called his name, but she hadn't had much time for him lately. Why should he make time for her?

Instead, he crouched on a low closet shelf on top of a pile of fresh-smelling linens. He often wished he could hop inside one of the machines, especially on winter days, because everything came out toasty warm. It made violent thumping sounds, though, so he always resisted the temptation, even when a door stood open invitingly.

The cat watched a small, ragged hole in the wall near the floor, where the scent of mice lingered from long ago.

When he heard his human call his name again, he scrunched backward to stay hidden. His rump pressed against the hole in the wall. Suddenly, the wall gave way. He yowled in alarm as he fell backward.

He hoped he hadn't given away his location. He waited, listening.

The chattering female humans left, closing the door behind them. His human had left him behind. Again.

This time, the cat didn't mind. He had discovered many hidden rooms in the big house. Some he revealed to the humans, but others he kept as his personal hidey-holes. This new space was dusty and veiled with cobwebs. When he sneezed, he considered that it might not be worth exploring. He would have to groom himself after every visit.

The cat shook himself, sending up a cloud of dust motes, and began to leave.

Then he noticed the ribbon.

7

When Faith and the others walked out of the manor, a limo was waiting for them.

The driver opened one of the back doors and helped the women inside with a broad smile. He was a portly gentleman with ruddy cheeks and a bushy mustache.

Faith accepted the driver's steadying hand and sat next to Brooke.

Charlotte sat directly behind the driver and asked him if he knew the way to the restaurant.

"Yes, Mrs. Jaxon." The driver had the strong accent of a native New Englander. "I took a guest to the hospital across the way from it yesterday, so I know the best route."

"The hospital?" Charlotte frowned. "Is the guest all right?"

"He's right as rain." The driver twisted around in his seat to face Charlotte. "Damian, one of Mr. Foille's staff, was visiting a relative in the hospital."

Faith knew she should stay out of it, but she told herself she was merely following up on a lead the police might not know about. "What time was that?"

The driver glanced at her. "Around eleven. I brought him back around two thirty." Then he closed a clear privacy panel. He put the car in gear and began the drive to Boston.

Faith leaned back in her seat, puzzling over this new clue. When Officer Rooney questioned Lois in the library, Faith had surmised that Lionel had been killed between two and six. This new information brought Damian back to the manor in time to commit the murder.

"Are you working on another mystery?" Brooke asked, nudging Faith's arm.

Eileen leaned across the aisle. "You can't leave the book club out of it."

"That's right," Midge said. "We gals work as a team."

"What are you talking about?" Jenna asked. "What team? You have to let me in on this."

"The primary aim of the book club is reading and discussing fiction," Eileen said. "We've also had the opportunity to investigate a few real-life mysteries."

"Like when I was accused of murder," Midge added. "The girls came to my rescue, solving the crime and proving my innocence."

"Sometimes our animal companions help," Brooke said. "It's mostly Watson with his curiosity, but my angelfish did their part on one case."

The ladies explained to Jenna some of the other mysteries they'd helped to solve.

"I think that's partly what brought our children together," Charlotte told Faith's mother. "They've both helped solve mysteries, just like Frank Hardy and Nancy Drew."

The ladies shared a good-natured laugh.

"Okay, let's get to business." Midge lowered her voice. "First, how did Lionel pass?"

"From the questions Officer Rooney asked Lois this morning," Faith said, "I'm certain he didn't die from natural causes. And I noticed what appeared to be a smear of dirt or blood on his head when he was discovered on the biogas generator."

These comments created a flurry of questions from the other women.

By the time they entered Boston, Faith had told them about the time frame for the murder and was on the topic of suspects. The police seemed to consider Lois a potential killer, although Faith had thought she seemed genuinely surprised by Rooney's questions. Then there were the gardening gloves, one of which was stained, but Lois claimed they weren't hers.

"Some people are good at hiding their guilt," her mother said.

"And their secrets. Martin told me many times about people who were so adept at lying that only rigorous police work exposed the criminal."

"Are you saying not to count Lois out?" Jenna asked.

"Don't count anyone out," Mom said, surprising Faith. "Not until all the facts are in."

Faith was pleased that her mother and sister had jumped right into their investigation. A mystery turned out to be a great icebreaker, as all the women asked questions and tested theories. Though fancy hats were hardly what one envisioned when experienced detectives put their heads together to solve a mystery.

"Hannah Windmere told me she almost lost her organic farm because of Lionel," Faith said.

"That's a strong motivation for murder," Brooke said.

"What about Damian?" Midge asked. "He was only accounted for from eleven to two thirty. The driver says he was in Boston at a hospital, but he was back at the manor well before six. Which means he had plenty of time to do it."

"But what's his motivation?" Charlotte asked. "Why murder your employer and end your paycheck?"

"Damian became upset and ran out of the garden when Lionel introduced the new rose. Maybe he wasn't happy about the announcement for some reason." Faith paused, considering how that could give Damian a motive to kill, but she came up empty.

"He could have gotten a text message about the person he visited in the hospital," Eileen said.

"That makes more sense," Faith responded. "But I didn't notice him checking his phone."

The privacy panel slid open, and the driver announced, "We're almost there."

Charlotte raised her hands. "Ladies, I have a request. Let's forget about this mystery for the time being. We have a very important task to attend to during our luncheon."

"We have to work?" Brooke asked. "I thought I escaped the lunch rush."

The women laughed.

"I wanted this to be a surprise, Faith," Charlotte said. "We're going to have the wedding catered so the manor staff can enjoy the reception. I know Brooke won't be able to resist checking on things in the kitchen if she's responsible for the meal."

"That's true," Brooke said. "I want everything to be perfect for Faith and Wolfe's wedding."

The car stopped in front of a well-known French restaurant, but Faith had never dined there. It was way out of a librarian's price range, even one with the Jaxons' generous pay.

"We're going to have a tasting today for my top catering choice," Charlotte continued, motioning to the restaurant. "Of course, the final decision will be up to Faith and Wolfe."

Everyone agreed it was a great idea.

None of the women seemed to notice Faith was quiet. She agreed that Brooke and her staff should not cater the wedding, but she thought of her father's concerns about the cost. Wolfe's family had plenty of money, but her dad seemed prepared to pay for her wedding, as he had for Jenna's.

Perhaps it could be catered by a Lighthouse Bay restaurant instead. The Captain's Table was upscale and offered delicious meals. But she realized a small restaurant might not have the staff or experience to cater a wedding the size the Jaxons seemed to want.

Rather than ruin an outing the rest of the ladies seemed eager to experience, Faith decided to give Charlotte's choice a chance. She could voice her concern about the cost later.

After the women exited the car, a man in a suit met them at the entrance and guided them to a private seating area.

While her friends and family oohed and aahed over the plush decor, Faith clutched her hands together in her lap. Another worry occurred to her. Jenna might feel upstaged by Faith's elaborate wedding plans.

Her mother reached for Faith's hands, her warm touch easing Faith's nerves. "What's wrong, honey? I'm certain the food will be great. I've read about this restaurant in travel magazines."

"I'm feeling a little out of my league," Faith whispered.

"Nonsense. You deserve this."

Faith watched Jenna, happily chatting with Brooke, Eileen, and Charlotte. Midge was testing her French by translating the menu. No one else seemed uncomfortable. She forced herself to relax. They probably wouldn't end up using this caterer anyway. It would be too expensive, and her father would talk them into a more modest arrangement. She might as well enjoy herself.

The waitstaff brought the first selection, small samples of appetizers that melted in Faith's mouth. The savory flavors of fresh herbs mingled with seafood, artfully arranged slivers of meats, and rich cheeses.

Faith forgot about the expense, the murder, and her absentee cat while she enjoyed the most delicious food she had ever tasted.

Next to Brooke's, of course.

The leather straps wrapped around the wooden box might have provided entertainment, but when the cat batted them, they were stiff with age.

So he turned his attention to a lid that stood open several inches. Dangling from the opening was an enticing loop of ribbon. He tugged on it. It was connected to something inside. He pulled the ribbon, freeing it and the stack of envelopes it bound together. Both smelled strongly of dust and faintly of earth.

The packet of envelopes made a fun rattling noise when the cat tossed it across the small room. He pounced on it, sending up a cloud of dust. This would not work. He dragged the packet out of the hidey-hole.

When he wiggled through the mouse hole, now plenty large enough for a cat, he trailed dust and cobwebs across the clean linens. He waited by the closed door.

At last, a human carrying a bundle of towels stepped inside.

The cat grabbed his new toy and dashed past her legs.

If he left his playthings in the big, sunny rooms on the third floor, they often disappeared. He would take his new find to the cottage he shared with his human. He managed half his grooming ritual before the door to the stairs opened. He snatched up his toy and darted through, causing a human to emit startled sounds.

The cat carried the rattle toy in his mouth by the ribbon. He worked his way awkwardly down the stairs to the second floor.

After all that work, he deserved a break, so he batted the toy around the hallway, pitching, chasing, then pouncing. The second floor was an enticing maze of hallways and rooms. He didn't pay much attention to where he was going. He focused on honing his hunting techniques as the toy rattled and bounced.

When the hallway ended, he picked up his toy. He was ready to go to the cottage for a nap in his favorite sunbeam on the back of the couch.

A tall human opened a door and paused, watching the cat. "What do you have there?" The person knelt beside him and stared at the rattle toy. "Where did you get that?"

There was only one, and he wasn't sharing. He tossed the toy across the hallway, then chased after it.

The tall human followed him and snatched the toy away before the cat could sink his teeth into the brittle paper.

"No," the person whispered. "It can't be. I'm certain these envelopes weren't in the box." He leaned down to pat the cat on the head. "I'm afraid I can't let you play with this. It's far too valuable." He stood quietly for a moment. "I need time to figure out what to do," he muttered and stepped back inside his room.

The cat meowed in protest, but there was no one to hear.

Finally, a different door opened. The lady with the wheels rolled into the hallway. "There you are, Mr. Watson! I've been looking all over for you. It's time for lunch."

He jumped onto her lap, and they wheeled to the magic box that transported them to the first floor.

"I'll have to spend extra time at the gym tonight." Jenna patted her stomach. "That food was delicious but so rich."

The others agreed.

As they stepped out of the restaurant and into the waiting limo, Faith briefly thought of asking the driver to take her to the hospital so she could verify Damian's alibi.

But as she mulled over the situation, she knew it was pointless. How could she discover who he visited? The patient might have a different last name than Damian, and he or she could have been released by now. And hospital personnel would never give her information on patients. The best she could do was mention his trip to Officer Rooney.

"Faith, why are you so quiet?" her mother murmured from beside her. "Didn't you like the food? We don't have to go with that caterer. This is your day."

The rest of their entourage was engaged in lively conversation. Faith shook herself out of her introspection. She didn't want to darken the upbeat mood in the car. "The food was wonderful. I'm sure I'll feel better when I see Watson."

"I understand," her mom said. "Animal companions have a way of easing our anxiety. I'm glad you have that handsome little cat in your life."

I hope I still do. It was beginning to feel as if a sweet lady in a red wheelchair had stolen Watson's heart.

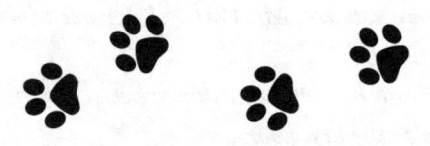

After parting ways with the ladies in the manor lobby, Faith returned to the library to relieve Laura. "Thanks for holding down the fort. How did it go?"

"It was pretty quiet," Laura reported. "No one wanted to miss a fantastic meal, and most of the guests went to outdoor sessions afterward. The weather is too nice to spend inside. How was your lunch?"

"Amazing." Faith described a few of the dishes to Laura.

"That sounds delicious, but sometimes all I want is peanut butter and jelly." Laura gathered her notebook and textbooks and left.

When Faith was alone in the library, she threw herself into work. A note reminded her to research Jeremiah's rare book. She decided to start locally and work her way out. It wasn't in the Castleton Manor collection or the Jaxons' private library. She checked the Candle House Library's online catalog, then e-mailed specialty bookstores in the Boston area.

Betsy rolled through the doorway in her red wheelchair. Her pink cheeks dimpled in a smile, giving her a vigorous, youthful look.

Watson trotted behind her.

8

Faith remembered calling for her cat before the luncheon. He hadn't been on the third floor after all. He had been with Betsy again. Faith resisted the irrational urge to snatch her cat away from Betsy and lock him in the cottage.

Watson hopped onto a chair in front of the fireplace and curled up for a nap. Faith could only hope he stayed in the library when Betsy left.

"How may I help you?" Faith asked, adopting her most pleasant and professional tone.

"I wanted to tell you how much I've loved spending time with Mr. Watson," Betsy replied. "I'm more of a dog person, but this cat is so wonderful that I could almost be persuaded to take a drive on the feline side of the road." She laughed.

"Watson is a special cat," Faith agreed.

Betsy's face abruptly crumpled into sorrow. "I had a darling little Maltese who passed away recently. Skipper was such a love, and I miss her so much."

"I'm sorry for your loss." Faith chided herself for her earlier selfish thoughts. Normally, she wasn't jealous when Watson made new friends. In fact, she was proud of the way he comforted others when they most needed it. And it sounded like he was helping Betsy heal from her recent heartache.

"I'm not one of those people who can plug the hole in my heart with a new dog. Not right away. I needed some time to mourn and heal." Betsy's expression changed back to sunshine. "Mr. Watson has helped me realize I might be ready for a new companion. I'll start the search when I return home."

"That's wonderful news." It suddenly occurred to Faith that Betsy had lost her Maltese, and Lionel's Pomeranian had lost his human. It was an obvious solution, but it needed a delicate approach. Besides, Lionel's family might yet claim Patches.

"But enough about that," Betsy continued. "May I take books from this library to my room?"

"Yes," Faith said. "Guests can check out books that are in general circulation. But rare books have to stay in the library."

Betsy gave Faith the title of a Dorothy Gilman spy mystery recommended by Lois.

As Faith checked the electronic catalog on her computer, she asked, "You found the box full of Lois's novels, didn't you?"

Betsy's face lit up. "That was so exciting. I'm saving the series to read in my patio garden at home. I need a different book while I'm here. If I don't read a few chapters in the evening, I can't sleep."

"I often read to calm down after a busy day," Faith admitted. "Although some books have kept me up past bedtime."

"I agree," Betsy said. "A real page-turner is hard to set aside. I'll tell myself to read just one more chapter, and the next thing I know, I've finished the book and it's three in the morning."

Faith laughed and handed the Gilman novel to Betsy. "I hope you enjoy it."

"Thank you." Betsy tucked the book into her tote and wheeled out the library door.

Watson jumped off the chair. For a moment, it seemed like he was going to follow Betsy, but he turned his attention to Faith instead, twining around her ankles and purring.

Faith reached down to rub his head. "You finally remembered me."

He hopped back onto the chair and curled into a ball again.

When Faith locked up the library late that afternoon, Watson followed her home to the cottage. At least the problem of the missing cat had been solved. Now she could concentrate on the wedding.

And the murder.

That evening's dinner was to be served in the banquet hall. Faith's parents accepted her offer of a home-cooked meal instead.

By the time her parents returned to the cottage after the last event of the day, Faith had dinner in the oven. The smell of chicken and potatoes filled the kitchen.

"We've had a lot of rich food this visit," her mother said. "I'm looking forward to simple dining."

"And saving a few bucks." Dad picked up the newspaper and sat in a chair in the living room. "Some folks may be able to spend money like there's no tomorrow, but the rest of us are on a budget."

Faith had not often heard her father talk about finances. His pay as a police officer had been modest, but her parents had budgeted and invested wisely. She wondered if they were having money problems. *One more worry.*

"We have enough to live comfortably, which is more than a lot of people can say," her mother said gently. "After that amazing lunch, I'm not even sure I can eat dinner. And don't worry." She patted Dad's shoulder. "Charlotte paid for the entire meal."

"How was the food?" he asked.

Her mom raved about the delicious food for several minutes, giving a glowing review of each dish. "I don't see how we can do better than Charlotte's choice for caterer."

"We can go cheaper," her father muttered as he flipped a page. "That would be better."

"What about the country club?" Faith asked. "Surely it's less expensive. How was your lunch?"

"Terrific," he replied. "They know how to grill the perfect burger."

What Faith really wanted to know was what her father thought of

Wolfe after spending the afternoon with him. She broached the topic carefully. "How was the golfing?"

"Blake won," her dad said. "I get the impression he's a bit of a rich playboy. I'm glad Wolfe has a good career."

Dad respected hardworking people, so Faith accepted his remark about Wolfe as a compliment.

When the oven timer went off, Watson beat Faith and her mother into the kitchen. He made a beeline to his empty food bowl, then glanced up at them.

"I'll get the food," her mother offered. "You'd better feed your cat."

Faith laughed as she poured kibble into Watson's bowl and refreshed his water.

He eagerly ate his dinner while Faith and her parents sat down to a meal of baked chicken breasts, asparagus, and fingerling potatoes. They talked about the afternoon's sessions.

After dinner, Faith picked up her bag. "Do you want to come to the book club meeting with me?" she asked her mother.

"If it's all right with you, I'll pass. I'm in need of a quiet evening with your father." Mom yawned. "I may turn in early tonight."

Watson planted himself in front of the front door.

Faith called over her shoulder to her parents, "I'm taking Watson."

When she opened the door, he bounded out to her car.

She smiled. It was good to have Watson back.

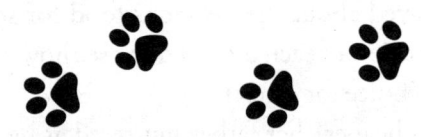

As wonderful as her parents were, Faith was ready for an evening with the book club. Being caught between her father's concerns about finances and her mother leaping on board with Charlotte's wedding plans was giving Faith a bad case of nerves and a bit of a headache.

She walked inside the Candle House Library with Watson at her heels and found her friends gathered around the stone fireplace that had originally been used to process tallow for candles. After being dressed up for Charlotte's luncheon, everyone had opted for casual clothing tonight, with shorts, capris, and T-shirts making up most of the apparel.

Midge's Chihuahua, Atticus, was dashing in a pale-green doggy jacket, and he wore Doggles, special eyeglasses to improve his failing vision. The dog scampered over to Watson, but the cat ignored him as usual.

The women helped themselves to tea and cookies from Snickerdoodles Bakery & Tea Shop, then sat down in the comfy chairs arranged around the fireplace.

"Did everyone finish the book?" Eileen asked. She removed her latest knitting project from her bag and immediately went to work.

Faith pulled her copy of a gardening-themed mystery from her bag, and for the next blissful hour, she discussed a good story with her friends.

"Next month's selection will be the third book in Lois Girten's series, since we've all read one and two," Eileen declared. "Thank you, Faith, for reminding us about her entertaining mysteries. It sounds like there will be plenty more in her series."

Lois had complained about Lionel ruining her career, but she had announced during one of the sessions that she had recently signed a three-book contract with her publisher to continue the series.

"Suggesting her might have been a little lazy, since I was already thinking about her because of the retreat," Faith said. "I've had a lot on my plate."

"I'll say." Brooke slid her book into her tote bag. "Planning a wedding, then having work interrupted with a murder. I'm amazed you remembered to suggest anyone."

The respite from talking about murder and the wedding ended as the ladies jumped to the very topics Faith had enjoyed forgetting for the past hour.

"I need to send Charlotte a thank-you card," Brooke continued. "I never would have had the chance to eat at that restaurant if she hadn't taken us. That chef is amazing."

The women compared notes on which dishes they preferred, as if the decision to use the restaurant as the wedding caterer were a done deal.

Which it might as well be, she thought moodily. Faith wondered what was wrong with her. Family and friends who loved her were thrilled to plan a wedding worthy of a princess. She should be a little more grateful.

Her mood refused to cooperate, so Faith decided to change the subject. "What a coincidence that Damian went to the hospital in the same neighborhood as the restaurant."

"I hope whoever he visited is okay," Midge said. "You gals told us he tore out of the garden Monday morning."

"So if he went to Boston around eleven and came back to the manor at two thirty, he had time to kill Lionel," Brooke reminded them.

"And part of Lois's story checks out." Eileen lowered her knitting needles. "I saw a notice for an author book signing in Glynde. Lois was scheduled to be in the bookstore from four to six."

"That confirms what she told Officer Rooney," Faith said. "How long does it take to drive from the manor to Glynde?"

"About fifteen minutes," Eileen said.

"That's not long enough to clear her," Brooke said. "So is Lois still on the suspect list?"

Faith nodded. "And then there's Hannah. I've learned a lot about Lois's schedule, but where was Hannah at the time of the murder?"

Eileen tucked away her knitting and stood. "I'm certain our police department is asking all the right questions. Faith, you need to keep your mind on your wedding. It's only a few weeks away."

Faith wasn't confident she could take her aunt's advice. Not when the murder had hit so close to home. At least her cat had returned.

Faith automatically glanced around the large room, which was growing dim as the sun set. "Where's Watson?"

The cat strolled down a hallway, his nose searching for the telltale sign of rodent invaders. Mice could wreak havoc on the books his human and her friends loved. While he didn't understand the appeal of books, he did enjoy chasing pests.

A door that was slightly ajar released faintly musty smells. Old things often attracted mice. He pushed the door with his shoulder.

"You startled me," the shaggy-haired man said. "I didn't see how late it was. Mrs. Piper will be running me out of here any minute."

The cat rubbed against the man's legs. It was a friendly gesture designed to bring him closer to the bird perched on the man's shoulder.

The bird aimed one round orange eye his way and ruffled his brown-and-white speckled feathers.

The human glanced down at the cat. "Please forgive Sage's manners. He had a bad experience with a cat once. That's why he can't use one wing." He stroked the bird's head with a finger. "See, Sage? The nice kitty came to say hello. He doesn't want to eat you."

While his intentions were not so pure, the cat had to admit that the bird's sturdy beak and curved talons appeared dangerous.

He was saved further dilemma concerning the bird's fate when his human entered the room. "Here you are, Watson."

"Thank you for recommending the Candle House Library archives," the man said.

"Did you find the book you wanted?" his person asked.

"No, but there are several terrific old horticulture books. One has an extensive excerpt from the book I'm looking for. With all the bits and pieces, I might be able to reconstruct parts of the book, even if I never find it."

The humans made more noises about books, but the cat's attention was drawn to a hole gnawed in the baseboard. He sniffed, but the inhabitant had moved on long ago. That reminded him of his new hidey-hole in the manor. He bumped against the baseboard and pawed at the hole, but nothing gave way.

His human's relative peeked inside the room. "I need to lock up."

The cat was glad. He had found nothing of interest. Besides, the bird glared at him as if it made snacks out of fellows like him. He put the bird with the large orange eyes in the category of "nice to dream about but unobtainable."

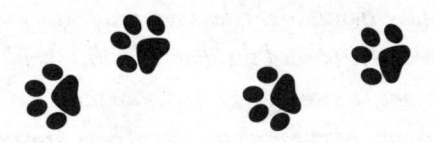

Faith picked up Watson. She wasn't letting him wander away again.

Eileen followed them to the front door. After Jeremiah exited, she held Faith back. "I noticed you were quiet while the ladies were discussing lunch. If you didn't like the food, you should let Charlotte know. She'll understand."

Faith hesitated a moment too long.

"What is it?" Eileen asked. "Are you having doubts about the wedding?"

"No, of course not," Faith said. "Marrying Wolfe is a dream come true. I just feel, well, like the wedding plans are spiraling out of control. Plus, Dad has been making comments about expenses. I'm certain he thinks the Jaxons are too extravagant. He feels like he should pay for the wedding as the father of the bride, but he can't afford their tastes."

"Your father has been acting pensive," Eileen mused. "Perhaps his mood is because you're the last child to marry."

"But I'm older than Jenna," Faith said. "The baby of the family has already married and has a son."

"Still, as long as a child is single, parents can think of themselves as more youthful than perhaps they are in reality. The fact that both daughters will now be married may be a lot for your father to absorb. He has to face the fact that his life is entering a new phase."

"Is that how you felt when Eric married?" Faith asked.

"I did when my son first told me about the engagement. But it wasn't long before I realized what a wonderful addition Claire was to our family. I understand your father's feelings, though. You're like a daughter to me. And a best friend. I know we'll stay close, but soon you'll be occupied with your husband and eventually a family."

Faith felt her face flush with embarrassment. She had been dwelling on her own problems without realizing how her life changes affected others.

"Do you think Mom and Dad are having financial problems?" Faith related her father's repeated comments about spending money, knowing her aunt would keep private family matters to herself.

"I hardly think so. They're too sensible. Although what previously seemed like plenty might feel small compared to the Jaxon fortune."

"Now I know how the heroines in Jane Austen novels felt," Faith said. "The woman of modest means marrying into a family of wealth and title."

"Oh, we should read another Austen novel in book group," Eileen said, her eyes lighting with excitement.

"Brooke would be overjoyed," Faith said. As a lover of romance books, Brooke was especially fond of Jane Austen.

Faith and Watson walked Eileen to her car in the parking lot.

As she drove home, Faith considered all her aunt had said. Mom was on board with an extravagant wedding, but Dad was upset about money and might be having anxiety about his last child marrying.

How can I possibly make both my parents happy?

9

Wednesday morning, Faith received an e-mail from a small shop in Boston specializing in Colonial American books. Amazingly, they had the horticulture book Jeremiah wanted, but it wasn't cheap. She forwarded the information to him.

Jeremiah answered her e-mail immediately, asking if he could have the book shipped to the library.

As she replied affirmatively, Faith found it curious that Jeremiah's relatively primitive lifestyle allowed for expensive antique books and same-day shipping.

Her musings were interrupted by guests seeking help solving the day's hidden treasure clue.

Rose had read a quote from *The Secret Garden* at breakfast. "'The secret garden was not the only one Dickon worked in. Round the cottage on the moor there was a piece of ground enclosed by a low wall of rough stones.' Today's treasure is hidden outdoors on the manor grounds."

The grounds covered acres of land. When pestered by guests for clues, Faith gently suggested people study the passage Rose had quoted.

"I love *The Secret Garden*, and I've read it at least half a dozen times," a young woman with long black hair said. She carried a small calico cat. "But there is no moor on the Castleton Manor grounds."

"Think about the quote," Faith said.

"It's a vegetable garden," the older gentleman with a fondness for sweater vests said. "I already searched there but with no results. Is the clue the stone wall? Is there a garden here like that?"

Faith raised her hands in a gesture of surrender. "Even if I knew where the prize is hidden, I'm not allowed to give clues."

She was relieved when the two guests left to attend talks. Since no one else was browsing the shelves, Faith decided to close the library to attend a panel discussion of cozy mystery authors who used gardens as their settings.

Watson followed her at first, but when he spotted Betsy, he scampered after her wheelchair.

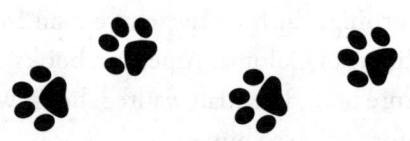

Guests sat on cushioned folding chairs in a pocket garden filled with the lush scent of blooming lavender.

Lois arrived at the last minute. Her dog seemed more subdued than usual. "I apologize for being late," she said. "I took Reynard for a brisk walk. Hopefully, he'll sit quietly during the discussion."

Guests nodded and smiled, probably feeling more comfortable around the rowdy dog now that his human had worn him out a little.

One panelist did not look convinced, his face creasing in a frown.

Probably not an animal lover, Faith thought.

The discussion was lively and interesting. Each writer displayed photos of gardens that inspired his or her stories. One author's work prominently featured a Japanese Zen garden. Although stark compared to a Castleton Manor flower garden, the traditional rock garden had a serene beauty and was well suited for dry regions. Another used an infinity pool as the instrument of death.

Faith was amazed by the variety of environments and gardening styles. She jotted down notes, determined to add several more books to her extensive to-be-read list.

During the question and answer session, the panel moderator pointed to one of the guests. "You're next, sir. What's your question?"

The portly gentleman held a pug in the crook of his arm. "Only one of you is a horticulturist by profession. Do you take liberties with the scientific facts regarding the details of the gardens?"

Lois's face flushed, and her mouth set in a hard line, as though she thought the question was directed at her. "We write fiction," she said, waving a hand to include the entire panel. "While authors strive to get the facts right, we do take creative liberties at times. And sometimes despite our best efforts, we make honest mistakes. In one of my books, I made a mistake by having pansies bloom in August."

The other panelists explained their research, describing when they stretched the facts to suit a plot and when readers pointed out their errors.

The discussion moved on to questions from other guests.

Faith remembered Lois's outburst the first day of the retreat. She had accused Lionel of ruining her career. Although she had experienced a setback, she seemed to be thriving now. Fans flocked to her as the panel ended, eager to chat with her and get her autograph.

As Faith left the pocket garden and crossed the lawn, she noticed Hannah hurrying toward the gardening shed. The police tape had been removed, and retreat speakers were giving talks on composting and gardening tools.

Faith managed to catch up to Hannah but only by breaking into a jog.

"Sorry but I'm in a rush," Hannah said. "My organic pest control talk begins in five minutes, and I barely have time to set up. If you want something, you'd better talk fast."

"This won't take long. Mr. Jaxon is interested in a biogas generator for the manor." That much was true. What Faith said next was stretching the truth a little, but she justified it as an attempt to place each of her suspects at the time of Lionel's death. "He wanted to talk to you about it on Monday, but he couldn't find you."

Hannah stopped. "I had an irrigation emergency on my farm, and I had to rush home to make sure the issue was addressed properly." She paused and studied Faith. "Why do you ask?"

"I was wondering if you're concerned that Lionel was found with his face over the hopper of your biogas generator," Faith said. "Maybe a competitor was trying to make it appear that your generator is unsafe."

Hannah took a step back, her eyes wide with surprise. "I hadn't thought of it that way. I only plaster my generator with warning labels to satisfy government regulations. It's completely safe."

"So you don't believe Lionel died from inhaling methane fumes?" Faith pressed.

"It's highly unlikely," Hannah answered. "He was an overweight older man who could have suffered from a heart attack or a stroke. Anything could have taken him out. And he just happened to be standing near the biogas generator when he expired."

"The police haven't released the cause of death, but you could be right. It doesn't make sense that Lionel would inhale methane fumes long enough to kill himself." Faith moved as though she were leaving, then turned back. "But then, why was he found with his face over the hopper?"

"I don't like to speculate about such unpleasant topics. I prefer to leave that kind of thing to the police. Please excuse me." Hannah hurried away.

Faith continued to the library. For the rest of the morning, patrons kept her busy, but work couldn't keep her mind entirely off the investigation into Lionel's death.

When Faith joined her parents in the Jaxons' private third-floor dining room for lunch, she was startled to see Watson stroll in from a hallway. She had seen him a short time ago with Betsy. Her cat certainly got around quickly.

"Well, look who's decided to grace us with his presence," her father said.

Faith's mother reached down to pet him. "Hello, Watson."

The tuxedo cat greeted each guest, then rubbed his face on Dad's trousers.

"Hey, buddy," her father said. "I'm not your personal towel."

"Watson is expressing his affection for you," Mom said. "It's what cats do."

"I don't think that's it," Dad responded. "He cleaned his face on my pants. You can see the gunk he left behind."

"Let me get you something to wipe that off," Charlotte said.

"I'll get it," Faith said. "He is my cat, after all." She hurried to the kitchen and returned with a damp dishcloth. She knelt and wiped her father's trouser leg clean, then examined what she had removed. "Odd. It's a cobweb. But the cleaning staff is so thorough. Where would he have found a cobweb?"

When Wolfe arrived, Charlotte and Faith's mother carried dishes from the kitchen to the dining room. Faith hoped her father noticed that Charlotte was not dependent upon a team of helpers. She was perfectly capable of making and serving her own meal.

After a light lunch of fresh garden salad and chicken sandwiches, Charlotte took Faith's parents to the private library to see a document pertaining to Dad's ancestor Josiah Newberry.

Faith and Wolfe cleared the table, carrying dishes to the kitchen. She had a rare moment alone with Wolfe. She was bursting with things to tell him, but she didn't want him to worry that she was involved in another murder case. *Does it count as involved if I can't find anything?*

Wolfe's handsome face creased with concern. "Are you feeling all right? Not having second thoughts, are you?"

Faith was about to marry this caring and perceptive man. Full disclosure was the best policy. "I'm incredibly happy and excited to be marrying you. It's the preparations that are bothering me. The wedding planning is a little overwhelming."

"Even though our mothers have clearly taken charge?" Wolfe asked, with a twinkle in his incredibly blue eyes. "Or is it because they've taken charge?"

Faith smiled. "I don't want to seem ungrateful, but honestly, I'd be happy if we had a small ceremony in the Victorian garden with a few close friends and family and a reception catered by Snickerdoodles."

Wolfe pulled Faith close and wrapped his arms around her. "Me too. And if that's what you really want, that's what we'll do."

"Really?" Faith asked. "I was going along with their plans because I thought it was what you wanted."

Wolfe released her, then took her hand and led her to the living room.

Watson pranced in and leaped onto the sofa, planting himself squarely in the middle before they could sit down.

"Okay, Watson," Wolfe said with a laugh. "You can sit next to Faith."

But that wasn't good enough for the handsome cat. To Faith's delight, Watson crawled onto her lap, curled up, and began purring loudly.

Wolfe scooted closer. "Before we break the news to our parents," he began cautiously, "I want to point out a few side issues. I'm the second son to marry in my family."

"And I'm the second—and last—child in mine."

"From my observations of my brother's wedding and weddings in general, the ceremony and reception are primarily for the benefit of the families involved."

"Well, yes," Faith said slowly. "I've heard that."

"A wedding is the ceremony that bonds two people for life. With that comes the bonding of extended families. Weddings often serve as a family reunion, bringing together people who rarely see each other."

Faith felt her heart sink. Wolfe's words were convincing. She also knew how disappointed the Jaxon and Newberry women would be to lose their excuse to plan a major event. Not to mention dressing up. They had gone all out for a caterer tasting.

"I can see your point," she said reluctantly. "It's not just about us."

"Unfortunately, no. But I have an idea about how we can alleviate some stress."

"How is that?"

"Give our mothers free rein. Let them plan the wedding any way they want, as long as we only have to show up for the ceremony."

"That does sound like an option." Faith's heart lifted a little at the idea. "Although if we relinquish all control, our mothers may schedule the ceremony in Windsor Castle."

They both laughed, and even Watson seemed to smile.

Wolfe kissed her forehead. "That's one of the reasons why I love you. You can make the best of any situation."

The moment was interrupted when Wolfe's cell phone chimed with a text message.

He checked the screen and jumped up. "It's from Marlene. She says it's an emergency."

10

Faith and Wolfe rushed from the third floor to Marlene's basement office, Watson at their heels.

Laura sat slumped in a chair at a round table in the center of the spacious office. When she glanced over her shoulder at Faith and Wolfe, her light-blue eyes were wide with fear. Faith hoped the young woman hadn't gotten into trouble with Marlene.

"I regret pulling you away from your busy day." Marlene sat at the table instead of at her usual post behind her desk. She was impeccably attired in a navy-blue suit. "Please take a seat. Laura insisted this was of the utmost importance."

Faith relaxed a little. If the meeting was at Laura's request, she probably wasn't in trouble. Wolfe and Faith took their seats and faced Laura.

"I was cleaning rooms," Laura began. "What our guests have in their rooms is their business, but I couldn't help noticing a stack of old envelopes in Mr. Winston's room. I mean, these were really old. Kind of yellowed and worn around the edges. They were tied together with a tattered ribbon. And they weren't like modern envelopes. They looked more like folded sheets of paper."

"During Lionel's announcement Monday morning, he mentioned an estate sale," Faith said. "That's where he found the heirloom rose. Maybe these have something to do with the rose."

"The Hortense Danford rose." Marlene nodded. "But Laura has more information to share."

Laura clasped her hands and rested them on the table. "So I thought they were old, and I was curious. But I wasn't snooping." She turned to Faith. "I saw your last name on the top envelope. 'Jane Newberry' was written in old-fashioned handwriting, along with an address. No zip code, of course. This was way before zip codes."

"Newberry isn't a terribly unusual name in New England," Faith said, but her curiosity kicked into overdrive about historical items that could be related to her ancestors. And it didn't escape her interest that Damian was once again on her radar. "The envelopes probably don't have anything to do with my family." *But wouldn't it be amazing if they did?* "Where are they now?"

"I didn't touch them," Laura said. "As far as I know, they're still in his room."

Faith began to stand. "I want to see them."

"That would create an awkward situation," Marlene said. "How could we explain our desire to enter his room to examine items that are none of our business?"

"Unless they have something to do with Lionel's death," Wolfe said.

"You mean I might have cleaned a murderer's room?" Laura asked in alarm.

"Let's not jump to conclusions," Marlene said. "I merely wanted to bring this to your attention because the envelopes were addressed to a Newberry."

"Don't you think it's peculiar that artifacts from the estate sale Lionel mentioned in the last speech of his life were found in his employee's room?" Wolfe asked.

"And that 'Newberry' is written on them," Laura chimed in.

"We don't know for sure that the envelopes came from that sale," Faith said. "Even if they did, Damian would naturally have access to materials used by Lionel. He might be researching the origins of the rose plant."

"You're right," Wolfe said. "We're speculating, both about where the envelopes originated and whether Jane Newberry is related to your family."

"I would still love to see what's in those envelopes," Faith said wistfully.

Marlene glared at her.

"Of course, I wouldn't dream of violating a guest's privacy," Faith added quickly.

"What if you are correct and the envelopes are somehow related to Lionel's death?" Marlene asked Wolfe. "Perhaps Laura should report this information to Chief Garris."

"I agree. It seems like a long shot, but that's not for us to judge." Wolfe stood. "And that's as far as this information should go."

Marlene and Laura voiced their agreement.

"Will you sit with me while I talk to the police?" Laura asked the assistant manager.

Marlene cast a benevolent—maybe even an affectionate—glance at the young woman. "Yes, I'll be right here."

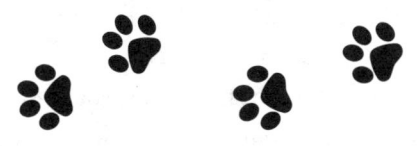

Faith didn't have long to think about the strange envelopes. Her talk on garden-themed mysteries was scheduled to begin soon.

When Faith arrived in the salon, guests were already filing in and taking their seats. She went to the podium and set up her laptop so she could project her presentation onto a freestanding screen. Watson sat on a nearby chair as if to offer moral support.

After everyone was seated, Faith took a deep breath. The doors to the balcony at her back were open, and a gentle summer breeze brought in the delicate scent of flowers. Smiling, she welcomed the guests and started her discussion of gardening amateur sleuths in classic tales and recently published novels. She began with Agatha Christie's Miss Marple.

When Faith finished her slideshow, the audience applauded.

"We have time for a few questions," Faith said.

Several hands shot up.

Faith pointed to the young woman with long black hair who held a calico cat in her lap. "Yes?"

"Not a question but a comment. With so many potential murder weapons, including poison and tools, I'm surprised more writers don't set their mysteries in gardens."

"Plus, there are plenty of places to bury a body," a man near her added, his bow tie jiggling with each excited word. "Newly worked soil is easy to dig in. Not to mention compost piles."

Faith was regularly amazed at the enthusiasm mystery readers had for puzzling out even the most gruesome crimes. "I hadn't thought of it that way."

Another hand rose.

"Yes?" Faith asked.

"Have the police released poor Mr. Foille's cause of death?" the elderly woman asked in a wavering voice.

"No," Faith said. She might have her suspicions and theories, but the Lighthouse Bay police had not released definitive information yet.

She was saved further questions when someone shouted, "I found it!"

Faith turned to the balcony overlooking the yard and saw a man grasping a long, thin object. He rushed through the French doors, then skidded to a halt, obviously startled to be on the podium side of an audience. Now that he was closer, Faith realized the object he held was a gardening hoe.

Several audience members gasped, and the man with the bow tie jumped out of his seat.

The man's face flushed red under deeply tanned skin. "Oh. I have come in the wrong door." His words carried a slight Spanish accent. "I am so sorry to interrupt."

"May I help you?" Faith asked.

The man eyed the hoe clutched in his hand. "I noticed this hidden behind the begonia pots under the nesting boxes for robins. Right where the first prize was hidden, beside the gardening shed. Not very imaginative." He frowned. "I was convinced I found the next treasure, but there are no books. Besides, the hoe seems to have been used. Now that I think about it, this can't be the prize."

Watson stood on his chair, his fur bristling and his stub of a tail puffing. Faith's cat had an uncanny ability to sniff out clues.

"Please wait a moment, and I'll help you sort it out," Faith told the man. She smiled at the audience. "Thank you for joining me today. Please drop by the library later if you need any help finding the books I referenced."

She waited for the audience to leave the salon before she introduced herself to the man and extended her hand.

He shook it. "I'm Eduardo Espinoza."

"It's strange that a hoe would be hidden behind flower planters," Faith commented.

"The manor gardens are immaculate," Eduardo said. "I assumed something out of place was a hidden treasure."

Faith inspected the gardening tool in his hands. *Foille Enterprises* was stamped into the wooden handle. On one end, she noticed a dark stain. "I need to call the police. They might be interested in seeing this tool. They'll probably have questions for you too."

Eduardo grimaced. "Do you think it has something to do with Lionel's death?"

"I don't know, but let's not take any chances."

"And now my fingerprints are all over the handle. I had no idea." Eduardo set the hoe down and wiped his palms on his pants.

Faith called the police and explained the situation to Officer Rooney.

While Eduardo waited, he called his wife to let her know where he was, then sat on a chair next to Watson's and scratched the cat behind the ears.

A few minutes later, his wife arrived, dressed in hiking clothes. They spoke quietly, staring at the hoe.

Faith had a few minutes to think. The mark on Lionel's head could have been made by a gardening tool. She thought it was unlikely the killer had attacked him, then placed him over the generator. Lionel was a large man. It made more sense that he had been leaning over the biogas generator's hopper when someone struck him from behind. Either way, the killer was probably counting on his death appearing to be from inhaling methane fumes.

Faith realized she had as much interest in solving the mystery as the nosiest guest. Wanting to bring a criminal to justice wasn't necessarily a bad thing, as long as the motivation wasn't from a ghoulish desire to have an insider's peek at the grisly details. After all, a killer might be on the loose at the manor.

Eban tapped on the side of the open balcony door, his work gloves in his free hand. "The police asked me to meet them in the salon."

"They should be here soon," Faith said.

Eban stepped inside, glancing at the couple who still murmured to each other while they patted Watson. "What's this about?" he asked Faith in a low voice.

"I'd better not say. From past experience, I know the police don't like people talking to each other until they have a chance to ask their questions."

Eban frowned. "It sounds serious."

"It could be," Faith said. "Or it might be nothing. We'll have to see what the police think."

Officer Rooney arrived with Officer Bryan Laddy. They wasted no time as they interviewed Eduardo.

After Eduardo and his wife left, Watson walked over to Faith while the police moved on to question Eban.

"Did you notice any hoes missing from the gardening shed?" Laddy asked.

"No, but there are dozens of tools in the shed," Eban replied. "A hoe could have dropped behind the begonia planters without anyone noticing."

Rooney gave the hoe to Eban. "Does it look familiar?"

Eban studied it, then shook his head. "The logo stamped on the handle says it's a Lionel Foille tool. He has a line of designer tools for home gardeners. But we use heavy-duty professional tools."

Faith didn't have much to add when they interviewed her.

After the police left, with the hoe wrapped carefully in paper and sealed with tape, she approached Eban.

"They think that hoe was used to murder Lionel, don't they?" he asked. He appeared a little pale beneath his summer tan.

"Maybe," Faith said. "It sounded like you couldn't help them much, but perhaps you can help me. Did you notice what time Hannah Windmere left the manor Monday?"

"After six," Eban said quickly.

"You seem certain."

"Her car was parked behind the riding mower I needed. I couldn't find her anywhere, so I had to work on other things. I went to the gardening shed several times that afternoon, and the car was still there. Finally, I went to sharpen my pruning shears at 5:50."

"How do you know the exact time?" Faith asked.

"I had an alarm set for a sprinkler in a pocket garden that doesn't have an automatic timer," Eban explained. "I turned off the water, then went into the shed to sharpen my shears. When I came out at 6:15, her car was gone."

Faith almost gasped in surprise. Hannah had told her she left the manor to tend to an irrigation emergency on her organic farm. How could she do that if her car was parked behind the gardening shed all afternoon?

Eban raised an eyebrow. "What's wrong?"

"I was under the impression Hannah was gone part of the day, but I must have misunderstood."

Eban's cell phone chimed. "I need to shut off another sprinkler. Let me know if you have any more questions."

Faith did, but she was certain Eban didn't have the answers she needed. Lois and Hannah each had motivation to murder Lionel, and Damian had reacted strangely to his announcement of the rose discovery and its name.

And Eban had just confirmed that all three could have been at the manor at the time of Lionel's death.

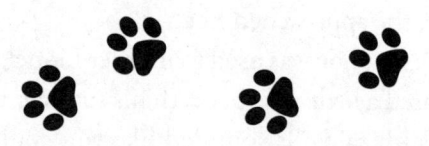

Faith slipped through the French doors in the library to attend an afternoon session about xeriscape landscaping, the technique designed to conserve water. She'd agreed to meet her parents at the talk, which was appropriately set in a succulent garden, featuring plants that were adept at retaining water in dry climates.

She tried to convince herself she wasn't going because Damian was on the panel. The week was flying by, and her goal of solving a murder had to be secondary to spending time with Mom and Dad. *But if I accomplish both at the same time, that's merely multitasking, isn't it?*

On her way to the garden, Faith saw Hannah and wondered if there might be a logical explanation for why the organic farmer claimed to have gone to her farm at the time of Lionel's murder while her car remained at the manor.

Faith caught up to Hannah, with Watson trotting behind. "Were you able to fix the irrigation at your farm?"

Hannah nodded. "I got there just in time to save a late planting of kale."

"That's good news," Faith said. "I was concerned because someone noticed your car didn't leave the parking area by the gardening shed until Monday evening."

"My car wouldn't start, so I caught a ride to my farm with Glenn Dobie," Hannah explained. "It's not far from here."

"I'm glad to hear that. I've got to run." Faith waved lightly and headed to the succulent garden with Watson still on her heels. When she was out of sight, Faith stopped, pulled out her cell phone, and called Glenn, the manor's boathouse keeper.

The phone rang several times before it went to voice mail. "This is Glenn. I'm fishing in New Hampshire, and I'll most likely be out of cell phone range. If this is a boathouse emergency—"

Faith listened while he rattled off the numbers for the boathouse as well as the front desk at the manor. Whether Hannah had told the truth about getting a ride with Glenn would have to wait until he returned.

The succulent garden was surrounded by a low wall of rough-hewn stones. This had to be the location of the third hidden treasure, judging by the description in *The Secret Garden*. None of the guests attending the talk seemed to be searching for it. Faith fought the temptation to drop a hint to her parents.

Faith found her parents already seated. She sat down next to her mother, and Watson hopped onto Faith's lap. It was amazing that she had once taken such a simple thing for granted. Now she felt special whenever he chose to join her.

Rose introduced Damian, and he took the podium. As he spoke about xeriscape landscaping, he exuded confidence. He certainly didn't look like a cold-blooded killer, but Faith knew appearances could be deceiving.

At the end of the discussion, the audience applauded.

Suddenly, a blond man in a bright Hawaiian shirt jumped out of his seat and dashed over to a thick cinquefoil shrub.

The other guests murmured with concern.

The man extracted a huge basket and a trio of long-handled gardening tools from the shrub. "I found the third treasure! Authentic Lionel Foille tools."

Guests crowded near the man to see what he had discovered.

Dread sank into Faith's bones as she was reminded of the authentic

Lionel Foille tool that might have been used to kill him. Lionel had several enemies at the retreat. Any of them could have owned the man's branded tools. Who had hidden the lone tool now in police possession? These tools, obviously brand-new, were wrapped in green burlap and tied with a rustic bow. It was interesting that those were meant to be today's prize when another of them could have been a murder weapon.

"There are two gardening books as well," the prizewinner said as he dug through the wrapping. "Oh, and an autographed copy of Lionel's *Roses for Every Climate*." His expression changed from joy to sorrow. "This might be one of the last books he signed."

There was a moment of silence as the others reflected on that.

Then the mood lightened when one woman piped up, "What else?"

"Some police officer I am," her dad grumbled. "The treasure was right under my nose."

"You've got three more chances," Mom reminded him. She touched Faith's arm. "We're going to the next session."

"I'll see you later. I need to open the library." Faith and Watson returned to the manor.

As they walked through the Great Hall Gallery, Faith saw Lois standing next to the statue of Dame Agatha Christie with Reynard at her side.

Lois's lips moved silently, as though speaking to herself. Or to Agatha.

Faith shivered. Was the woman seeking inspiration for her next novel from the great mystery author ... or thinking up ways to escape a murder charge?

11

Faith debated whether to interrupt Lois's moment of contemplation as the author stood beside the statue of Agatha Christie. The gardening retreat had reached its midway point, and she was running out of time to find answers to Lionel's murder. She would have to risk a little awkwardness.

Faith took a deep breath and approached Lois. "I often talk to Ms. Christie myself."

Lois spun around. "Oh, you startled me. My nerves have been shot since day one of this retreat. I thought I'd have a relaxing time, surrounded by luxury. Silly me."

"I'm sorry," Faith said. "Is there anything I can do to make your stay more pleasant?"

Lois chuckled. "You can find Lionel's killer. Then maybe I'll stop being bothered by ridiculous questions from the guests." Her expression hardened. "Or humiliating interrogations by the police."

Reynard suddenly noticed Watson and tensed.

Faith hoped her cat would exercise discretion around the excitable dog.

Watson boldly stepped forward and touched his nose to the Shiba Inu's.

Reynard jerked his head back with a yip of surprise.

That was enough for Watson. He took off toward the nearest staircase.

Reynard yanked the leash out of Lois's hand and tore after the nimble feline.

Faith suspected her cat was not running out of fear. His stubby tail wasn't puffed. This was a game.

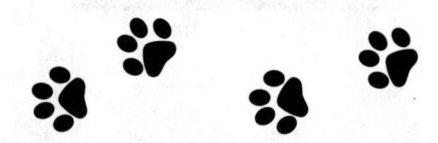

The cat led the dog and the humans on a merry chase across the lobby. He darted toward the safety of the staircase.

Typically, dogs couldn't keep up with him. He had the advantage of needle-sharp claws that gave him traction on the plush carpeting. However, this foxy-looking fellow was as swift as a cat.

The cat's heart pumped as he struggled to maintain his lead. He reached the top of the stairs and spied the door to the magic box closing. He darted inside.

The dog slid to a halt, nearly getting his nose pinched in the closing door of the magic box.

The cat smirked at him, then glanced up at the nice lady inside the box.

"Watson," she said, "you have impeccable timing."

The door opened on the top floor. He trotted behind her.

The nice lady walked into the living room carrying a rustling bag. She sat on the sofa and pulled out a feather toy. "Faith told me this is one of your favorites. I need to get in the habit of having toys around for my cat grandson."

She waved the feather around, allowing the cat to pounce on it, then snatched it away. She was pretty good at the game.

Then an annoying talking thing made a jangling noise. Humans always jumped to fetch it when it yelled at them. When she picked it up, he knew he had lost his playmate.

The cat trotted down the hall. Who needed humans? He had other means of entertainment. One of the doors was open a few inches. He stuck his paw into the crack and eased the door open.

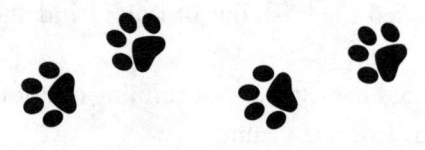

Lois caught up to her dog and grabbed his leash. "I'm so sorry. I hope Reynard didn't scare your cat."

Faith smiled. "If I'm not mistaken, Watson wasn't afraid. He was playing. I'm glad there weren't many people in the lobby. There should be no complaints about our two rascals."

"Another hassle is the last thing I need," Lois said. "Although the retreat has been more pleasant with the absence of a certain overblown TV personality."

Faith was startled to hear Lionel's death referred to in such a casual manner. She desperately wanted to ask Lois about the gardening glove with the suspicious stain. There was no subtle way to get the information she wanted, so she plunged ahead. "Did the police find out how those gloves made their way into your tote bag?"

"Obviously, I wore them to murder Lionel, then boldly carried them around practically in plain sight." Lois sighed. "That's what they think, anyway. In my murder mysteries, the killer never escapes. Why would I, of all people, take that risk?"

Faith checked her watch. "I need to open the library. Are you headed that way?"

"No, I'm changing shoes, then going on the maze tour." Lois glanced down at her dog as he wrapped his leash around her legs. "That way Reynard can expend some energy outdoors. He's going to be in the play later."

"Oh?" Faith thought having the energetic dog onstage in front of a crowd seemed like a bad idea, but it would be rude to say so. "Now I'm really excited to see the play."

"It'll be great," Lois said. "The kids do an excellent job."

Reynard seemed to have used up his limited supply of patience with human conversation. He bounced with puppy enthusiasm as Lois headed for her room.

As Faith walked to the library, she thought about Lois's objection to murder. It almost sounded as if she didn't mind the act itself, only the idea of getting caught.

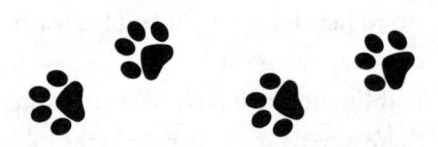

The cat crawled onto the bottom shelf in the little room. A piece of cardboard covered his secret hole. Some human had probably discovered it and tried to hide the opening from him. Cats were too smart for that. He poked his claws into the cardboard and tugged it out of the way.

At least they had left his hiding place alone. He nosed around, sneezed once, then examined the trunk, glad to see it was still there. The tall man had stolen his rattle toy, but maybe he could find a new toy inside the big wood and leather box.

He rested his paws on the edge of the box and peered inside. The only light reaching inside his secret room came through the enlarged mouse hole. He couldn't tell what treasures were hidden inside the box.

Nothing ventured, nothing gained. He leaped into the box and landed on a lumpy bundle of cloth.

The trunk wobbled. Frightened, the cat crouched to leap out of the box. Just before he jumped, the lid snapped shut, trapping him inside.

Huddling into a tight ball, he assessed his situation. The darkness was so complete, even his cat eyes could not see a thing. What was a cat to do?

Faith unlocked the library and made a beeline for her desk. She sank into her familiar chair with a sigh of relief. The library was her sanctuary, an island of calm when life became stressful.

Guests trickled in, keeping her occupied but not overwhelmed. Faith was grateful she had such a rewarding job. The lovely surroundings were a nice bonus.

Faith had just helped two guests find a gardening photo book mentioned in a session when a deliveryman entered the library. The young man wore a uniform shirt and shorts that exposed tanned, muscular arms and legs. His shoes looked suitable for walking many miles a day, and his shirt bore a logo for a private courier service.

As most first-time visitors did, the man paused to take in the splendor of the library. Then he approached Faith's desk. "I have a package for Mr. Jeremiah Fielding. Is he here?"

"Not at the moment. I'll contact him." Faith dialed Jeremiah's cell phone.

He picked up right away, and she told him that his book had arrived.

"Fantastic!" Jeremiah exclaimed. "I'm on a panel in a few minutes, so I can't come right now. Can you sign for it?"

"I'll be happy to, but maybe you should talk to the courier." Faith handed the phone to the young man.

After a brief conversation with Jeremiah, the courier gave the phone back to Faith. "You can sign for the package. But first you need to open it to check for any damage."

"Let me get my gloves." Faith set her phone on the desk and retrieved a pair of white gloves she used when examining rare books. She donned the gloves, then opened the shipping box. The book was protected with ample packing materials, which she was glad to see. She set the package on her desk, removed the wrapping, and peeled off the acid-free paper. "This should be in a museum."

In a museum exhibit of rare books, she had once seen an extremely valuable first edition of *Gulliver's Travels* by Jonathan Swift in a locked glass case. While Jeremiah's book wasn't worth anything near that, it had cost him plenty.

Faith carefully opened the leather cover and leafed through it. Other than the expected wear and aging of a volume from 1798, the book appeared to be in great condition. She signed the courier's form, and he left.

Faith started to repackage the book but realized this might be her only opportunity to examine a rare book from early American history. *Indigenous Farming Techniques of the Pennacook* was embossed on the cover, with the author's name below it.

Books of this era were often printed and sold with the pages bound in a manner that required the initial reader to separate them with a knife or other cutting tool. The thick pages of this volume had been cut, which meant the book had been read. Faith inhaled the pleasant musty smell of the old book.

The table of contents listed a chapter on the history of the Pennacook, which would be a treasure for Native American people tracing their ancestry to the tribe. As Faith gently thumbed through the book, she saw numerous drawings of the Pennacook with native flora and fauna. Other chapters discussed the geography of the region, weather, and finally the horticultural techniques that were of interest to Jeremiah.

One chapter title jumped out at Faith: "Medicinal and Poisonous Flora of the Region." It covered bittersweet nightshade, foxglove, and white baneberry.

"Excuse me."

Faith had been so entranced by the book that she hadn't noticed an older gentleman approach her desk.

"Yes?" Faith asked. "May I help you?"

"I'm trying to find the pet spa for Thor." The thin older man patted the head of a tiny Chihuahua cradled in his left arm. "But I'm totally lost."

After giving him directions, she decided she needed to repackage Jeremiah's book and remove the temptation to lose herself in study. If the gardener decided he didn't want the volume, Faith would offer to buy it for the Castleton Manor collection. She doubted he would relinquish such a treasure, though.

Laura arrived to give Faith a break. "It's quiet this afternoon."

The only two guests in the library sat in front of the fireplace, perhaps drawn there by the subtly aromatic flower arrangement.

"Some of the guests signed up for the tour of the living history museum," Faith explained.

"We went on a field trip there for one of my college classes," Laura said. "It really made history come to life for me."

"A book arrived for Jeremiah Fielding," Faith said. "He knows it's here in the library. The book is valuable, so I'll tuck it away in my desk."

Even inside the shipping box, the book fit easily in one of the deep drawers in the ornately carved desk.

"How valuable is it?"

"You don't want to know," Faith said. "But with a title like *Indigenous Farming Techniques of the Pennacook*, I doubt anyone will be tempted to steal it."

Faith told herself she wasn't investigating, but she couldn't resist peeking in on two of her suspects.

A panel discussion about gardening in small spaces featured Damian, Hannah, Jeremiah, and Eban. Damian had taken the place of his deceased employer on the panel, and Rose moderated it. The group shared a table in a pocket garden featuring miniature varieties of flowers.

Faith took a seat at the back, not wanting to disturb the discussion already in full swing.

Hannah, with her soft voice, laid-back manner, and casual batik-print tunic, still managed to dominate the panel as she spoke incessantly about the superiority of organic gardening methods.

"I'm sure we all agree that organic methods are preferable," Rose interrupted after a few minutes. "However, our audience is interested in learning how gardening techniques may be scaled down to small backyards, patios, and even apartment balconies. Eban, your employer's gardens are huge. How does your experience apply to our topic?"

Faith admired how Rose diplomatically steered the conversation back to the panel theme.

"I volunteer to create miniature gardens in retirement homes," Eban said. "The residents might have limited space, but they can still grow amazing tomatoes, peppers, and other vegetables, as well as annual and perennial flowers. I've seen entire gardens growing successfully in a single clay pot."

"That's wonderful," Rose said. "Jeremiah, you spend most of your time in the vast Maine woods. How does that make you an expert on growing in small spaces?"

"I enjoy gardening, but I don't want to do it by clearing the trees that are already in the forest," Jeremiah answered. "I have found that a few square feet of open space between trees can support a patch of corn or beans. You don't need acres of fields like modern commercial farms."

The owl on his shoulder hooted.

"As you can see, Sage agrees with me," Jeremiah said with a smile.

The audience laughed.

The discussion flowed as panelists described the importance of the right soil conditions and sunlight for tiny gardens.

Once again, Hannah brought up the superiority of organic gardening. "Pesticides equal poison," she said, her voice soft but insistent. "You must always use heirloom seeds. Hybrid seeds reduce the genetic pool. Genetically modified seeds are even worse."

Damian held up one hand. "I agree that in an ideal world those should be your choices. However, hungry people in developing countries appreciate having disease-resistant varieties of hybrid rice and wheat."

Hannah crossed her arms over her chest. "I won't compromise my beliefs."

Jeremiah jumped in. "I don't use pesticides, and I do use heirloom seeds. I also use row cover made from synthetic fabric to keep insects off my plants. Not all gardening innovations are bad, but we need to be careful that they don't create new hazards." He turned to Hannah. "Like your biogas generator, which killed Lionel."

12

A collective gasp escaped the audience.

Hannah's face flushed. "The biogas generator is completely safe," she said in a surprisingly calm tone. "The government requires warning labels, but the gas isn't concentrated enough to cause harm. The police haven't yet announced how Lionel died. In all likelihood, he just happened to be near the generator when he expired of natural causes."

"Then why are the police questioning people?" Jeremiah asked.

Several guests shifted in their chairs uneasily, but others seemed enthralled with the discussion.

Faith was relieved when Rose once again steered the panelists back on track with a question about the application of modern gardening techniques to small spaces.

At the conclusion of the talk, Rose fielded audience questions, then reminded guests about the high school performance of *The Secret Garden*.

"You don't want to miss the play tonight," Jeremiah said. "Sage has a starring role."

First Reynard and now Sage. Faith wondered if it was a good idea to have live animals in the play. Especially considering Reynard's last performance onstage.

Guests crowded around the table in the small garden. Faith waited for a young woman to finish chatting with Jeremiah before she approached.

"Do you have the book?" Jeremiah asked. "Can I see it?"

"It's in the library," Faith said. "I took a peek, and it seems to be in great condition for such an old volume. I had to tear myself away before I read the entire book."

"I'm hoping there will be information to help me identify medicinal and poisonous native New England plants," Jeremiah said. "I might have found a rare variety in the woods on the manor grounds."

"That's interesting," Faith said. "I hope the book is useful."

"I'll drop by as soon as I can to pick it up," Jeremiah promised. "It's been crazy today. Plus, I have to update my blog. Lots of new people signed up after my speech at the Monday banquet, and I need to keep the content flowing."

A guest approached, clearly eager to talk to Jeremiah.

Faith stepped back.

Hannah jumped up from the table, brushing against Faith in her haste to leave the garden. "Excuse me," she said.

When Faith moved to exit the pocket garden, she noticed Damian and Rose smiling and laughing. If Faith wasn't mistaken, they seemed to share a few sparks of mutual admiration.

Rose waved to Faith, motioning for her to join them. "Damian, have you met the Castleton Manor librarian?"

"No, although I have seen you around this week," Damian said.

"I'm Faith Newberry. I gave a talk earlier today, but I believe you were also speaking at that time." She offered her hand.

"Newberry?" Damian frowned as he clasped her hand. "That's an unusual name."

"It's not all that rare in New England," Faith said carefully. *It was on an old envelope a housekeeper found in your room, as a matter of fact.*

Damian glanced at his watch. "I didn't realize it was so late. I have to go. A family member is in the hospital in Boston. I want to squeeze in a visit before dinner tonight."

"I hope it's not serious," Rose said.

"The doctors gave Grandma Finch a good prognosis. She's a tough old bird. Her description, not mine." Damian slapped his palm to his forehead. "Oh no, I forgot to call for a car. I don't know if I can get one on such short notice."

"I'll call," Faith said. "We're happy to accommodate." As she dialed the front desk, she realized there were dozens of medical centers in the region. She shouldn't let a suspect know she'd been tracking his movements. "Which hospital?"

Damian gave her the name. It was the one near the restaurant Faith and her friends had tested to cater the wedding.

She walked ahead to make the call, and Damian and Rose followed. Faith loved how people with shared interests often connected at the manor events. A little guilt flushed her cheeks at her suspicion of Damian. Maybe she should warn Rose.

No, it's none of my business. Unless I find evidence, that is.

Arranging a ride for Damian took longer than Faith expected. When she finally walked through the library door, she stepped into chaos. Laura stood with her back against a bookcase as five guests hammered her with questions. They seemed to think that whoever spoke loudest would receive their answer first.

"I heard there are first editions of Agatha Christie's novels here. Where are they?"

"I need the book that man recommended in his talk. I can't remember the name of it, but it had a blue cover."

"Where's the book about how to grow roses in Arizona?"

Faith came to Laura's rescue. "First editions are on display in that case." She pointed to a locked glass bookcase. "Special viewings must be arranged in advance." She ushered the rose aficionado toward another bookcase. "The gardening books are on those shelves." Then she addressed the third guest. "Which talk? And who was the speaker?"

Laura stepped up and took care of the remaining guests.

When the patrons were satisfied, the library returned to its normal state of peace.

Laura slumped onto a velvet chair. "I'm not cut out to be a librarian." She lowered her face into her hands. "I totally blew it."

"You did not. They were being a little ridiculous." Faith patted the young college student's shoulder. "Let me give you a hint."

Laura glanced up, her eyes shining with tears.

"Before you feel overwhelmed, take your position here." Faith steered Laura behind the ornate desk. "This puts you in a position of authority. Guests will feel more inclined to stand in line and wait their turn. Go ahead. Try it."

Laura sat. She placed both hands on the desk and surveyed the library. "I never thought of it that way, but it does make sense."

By the time they had straightened up the large room, a new wave of guests swamped the library. Laura handled multiple questions with more poise from behind the desk. The rest of the afternoon flew by.

Faith closed and locked the door. "Thank you for staying." She smiled at Laura. "I couldn't have managed without you."

"Thanks for your advice. I almost feel like a real librarian."

"If we stay this busy," Faith said, "you'll be a full-time librarian soon."

Laura's pale face flushed with a shy smile.

When Faith opened her cottage door, she expected to be greeted by Watson, but he was nowhere in sight. She walked into the kitchen and found her father sitting at the table with a book.

He raised a finger to his lips. "Your mother went to put her feet up, but she fell asleep. I'm not going to wake her until dinner."

Faith sat in the chair opposite him. "I'll wake her in thirty minutes because she'll want time to get ready. We're seeing the high school play tonight. Attending the theater is always a good excuse to dress up, and you know how Mom likes to feel pretty."

He smiled. "Your mother is a beautiful woman, whether she's in a ballroom gown or a pair of blue jeans."

Faith returned her father's smile. "That she is."

Late afternoon sunlight streamed through the window. Sitting with her father, Faith felt a special contentment. She pulled out her notebook and jotted down notes about the murder of Lionel.

Her father stood to top off his coffee. "Can I get you a cup? It's decaf."

"Sure. Thanks."

As he set the mug in front of Faith, his gaze fell on her notebook. "I thought you were working on wedding plans."

"Finding out what happened to Lionel is more urgent. The guests leave in a few days." She set her pen on the table. "I need your expert opinion."

Dad glanced toward the doorway. "We can't let your mother know we're discussing a case."

"Mom joined in the book club's discussion of Lionel's death on the way to Boston."

"She probably thought of it as a parlor game. She warned me we're on vacation and that she expects me to avoid police work for the week. But I can't help thinking about the case. As pleased as I am that you're marrying a quality man like Wolfe, I'm tired of hearing about nothing but the wedding."

He had given her exactly the opening she'd been looking for all week. "I'll be blunt. I know you aren't happy with the elaborate plans Charlotte and Mom are coming up with."

"I don't want to rain on your parade." He sat beside her. "But I have a feeling it's not exactly your parade we're talking about."

"True. Wolfe and I would prefer to keep things simple. But he also pointed out that weddings are more for the families than for the bride and groom. Plus, the Jaxons have many social and business connections who expect to be invited."

Her father sipped his decaf, then set the cup on the table. "Since we're being honest, can I tell you something?"

"Go ahead. I want to know what you're thinking."

"I paid for Jenna's wedding, and I want to pay for yours too," Dad said. "But your mother and Charlotte keep adding on more and more. They're going way over what I had budgeted."

She'd been right. "Considering the Jaxon family fortune, no one expects you to bear the full expense of the wedding."

"It's not about money," he said. "It's tradition. The father of the bride pays for the wedding. I have always wanted to do this for you."

Faith placed a hand over her dad's. "Let's talk to Mom."

He shook his head. "She's having so much fun. And you're our last child to marry. I need to resign myself to a wedding worthy of Buckingham Palace."

"Oh, it's not that bad." Faith paused. "Okay, maybe it is."

They both laughed.

Faith felt like a twenty-pound boulder had been lifted off her shoulders.

Her father tapped Faith's notebook and whispered, "Got any theories?"

Faith shared her information about suspects and motivations. Lois and Hannah had professional grudges against Lionel. Hannah had an alibi, but it relied on Glenn, who wasn't home to confirm whether he'd given Hannah a ride to her farm Monday. Lois had only half of the window of opportunity accounted for with her book signing from four to six. Damian's reaction at the rose-naming announcement had been odd. He didn't have an obvious motive, but perhaps there was something they hadn't yet discovered.

As she spoke, she realized how flimsy her theories were. Even the time frame for the murder was weak. She was assuming she knew when it had happened according to Rooney's questioning of Lois, but she didn't know if it was accurate.

"I also haven't determined Jeremiah's whereabouts," Faith said. "When Lionel didn't show up for the banquet Monday night, he volunteered to speak. Jeremiah gained a lot of subscribers to his blog after his talk. That seems like a poor reason to kill a man, but maybe I should add him to the suspect list."

"People have killed for far less." Her dad pulled a notepad from his pocket. "I've been doing a little thinking on that topic too."

With his superior vision, the cat should have been able to see the interior of his prison, but not one speck of light penetrated the musty box. He huddled in the cramped space. Surely his human missed him by now. From the way his stomach rumbled, he knew it was past dinnertime.

He stood, using his claws to hold himself steady on the wobbly cloth-covered pile. He stretched his legs and pushed his arched back against the lid of the box. It wouldn't budge.

The cat yowled for the hundredth time. Realistically, how could any human, with their poor hearing, detect his pathetic mewing from inside a box that was inside a wall?

He curled into a tight ball, cuddling up against the cold, lumpy cloth. It was a poor substitute for his warm human.

After a wonderful meal in the banquet hall, Faith, Wolfe, Charlotte, and her parents followed the guests onto the loggia. Wolfe and her father chatted as they walked ahead of the women.

Faith searched the rows of chairs facing the lawn. "Do you see Betsy?" she asked.

Mom scanned the crowd. "No, I don't see her."

"She was in the banquet hall at dinner," Charlotte remarked.

"Did she have Watson with her?" Faith asked.

"Not that I noticed," Charlotte said. "Is he missing?"

"I haven't seen him since he and Reynard played tag across the lobby."

"Well, he followed me to the third floor earlier," Charlotte said. "But I didn't see him when I left for dinner."

"I'm sure he's here somewhere," her mother said. "Maybe he's avoiding the crowd."

Faith wanted to tell her mom that Watson loved a good party, especially when there were new animals to meet, but she didn't trust her voice. Maybe she was overreacting, but she was getting genuinely worried about her missing cat.

An older teenager stepped onto the stage. He was dressed in early 1900s attire—loosely cut trousers with cuffs, a straw boater hat, and a bow tie. "Good evening, ladies and gentlemen. Welcome to Lighthouse Bay High School's presentation of Frances Hodgson Burnett's classic children's novel *The Secret Garden*."

The crowd applauded.

"This production will run for one and a half hours with a brief intermission," he continued. "Afterward, please join us for a reception of tea, punch, and desserts in the Great Hall Gallery. And now, *The Secret Garden*." He bowed to the audience, then crossed the stage with the leggy, energetic stride of a teenager.

Her mom leaned close to Faith and whispered, "I can't imagine how they'll trim the book to just an hour and a half."

The production ended up being true to the story, even in condensed form. The young people acted with flair, attempting Yorkshire accents with amusing results. The character Dickon used both plush toys and live animals for his mobile menagerie. Lois's Shiba Inu managed to behave himself as he played the fox. Jeremiah's owl played the part of the crow.

At the end, the audience gave the students a standing ovation.

Guests filed back indoors where tables were set with crystal punch bowls, silver urns of hot water, selections of herbal teas, and a variety of desserts artfully arranged on tiered stands.

Faith couldn't imagine having room for one more bite after the delicious dinner she had so recently enjoyed, but the chocolate ganache cupcakes were too appealing to resist. She helped herself to one.

"The play was better than I expected," her father said.

"You must remember sitting through all those dance recitals and school plays Jenna and I were in," Faith said. "That must have been tedious."

"Nonsense," her mother said. "You girls were wonderful. So full of charm and talent."

Faith laughed. "I think every mother believes that."

"Anyway, it's different when you're watching your own kids." Her dad patted Wolfe's shoulder. "You'll find that out one day. This was still entertaining, even though I didn't know any of the actors."

"I thought it was clever to include our guests' pets," Charlotte said.

As the others chatted about the play and savored the desserts, a thought occurred to Faith, and a bite of cupcake stuck in her throat. Watson had stolen the show playing Alice's cat in the filming of a remake of *Alice in Wonderland* at the manor. He had been in the thick of things when a troupe of Shakespearean actors put on several plays there. Watson wouldn't miss the chance to be onstage again. So where was he?

Lois interrupted her thoughts. "Reynard deserves something extra for behaving himself tonight. Are there any dog treats?" The author wore a proud smile that melted the stress lines from her usually pinched expression. Her summer dress and stylish short hair gave her a fresh, youthful look.

Brooke walked over from where she was conferring with Marlene. "There are dog-friendly treats courtesy of Happy Tails Gourmet Bakery over there." She pointed to a small table, where a brightly colored bowl was decorated with paw prints and the words *Puppy Pastries*.

"Terrific," Lois said. "I was afraid Reynard would get too excited onstage when—"

A woman screamed.

Faith turned to see Hannah slip gracefully to the floor. A half-eaten shortbread cookie crumbled in her hand.

13

Faith rushed to Hannah's side as half a dozen guests pulled out cell phones to call 911. Perhaps Hannah was having an allergic reaction to the cookie she had eaten. Or maybe a bee, drawn inside by the flower arrangements, had stung her.

Hannah struggled to sit up, and Faith supported her shoulders. Her breathing was steady. She didn't seem to have trouble focusing on Faith's face. Perhaps the warmth of the summer night had merely caused the organic farmer to feel woozy.

"Faith." Hannah's eyelids drooped, and her breathing became labored. "This." She lifted a hand filled with cookie crumbles dotted with specks. "Lois Girten. Book four. Must be poisoned." Hannah closed her eyes and slumped against Faith.

Was Hannah accusing Lois of poisoning her? Faith could smell lavender. The specks on the cookie must have been herbs. Plenty of guests had sampled the desserts, but Hannah was the only one to become ill.

Within minutes, Faith heard the siren of an ambulance and saw flashing lights through the French doors lining the Great Hall Gallery.

The crowd made way as EMTs and police officers hustled inside.

Faith told Officer Rooney to save the cookie clutched in the organic farmer's hand. "Hannah implied that's what made her sick."

While the paramedics loaded Hannah onto a gurney, Rooney carefully bagged the crumbled remains of the lavender cookie.

Chief Garris pulled Faith aside. "I heard Ms. Windmere spoke to you before she passed out."

"Yes, she whispered to me." Faith paused, trying to remember Hannah's exact words. "She said, 'This,' then showed me the cookie that Officer Rooney collected. And she said, 'Lois Girten. Book four. Must be poisoned.' Then she lost consciousness."

"Book four?" Garris asked.

"That's a reference to a novel Lois wrote," Faith explained. "An herb must have been used to kill a character."

The chief scribbled notes on his notepad.

"There's something else you need to know," Faith said. "Jeremiah Fielding ordered an antique book. It arrived this morning. There's a chapter on poisonous native plants. But as far as I know, he hasn't picked it up yet. Still, that's coincidental, considering what just happened."

Garris had an uncanny ability to keep his emotions off his face, but Faith noticed one of his eyebrows lift subtly. "Don't repeat what Ms. Windmere said or this info about Mr. Fielding's book to anyone else. The last thing we need is a panicky crowd."

Faith nodded.

A few minutes later, the chief escorted Lois toward the door.

"Wait! I refuse to take Reynard to the police station," Lois protested. "It would be far too stressful for him."

"I suppose so." Garris waved to Faith. "Would you watch Ms. Girten's dog for a few hours?"

"Hours?" Lois repeated. "This is ridiculous! Do I need a lawyer?"

As Faith came near, Lois shoved Reynard's leash into her hand. Then Garris walked Lois toward a waiting police car.

Reynard gazed up at Faith and whined.

"What am I going to do with you?" she asked the dog. "You and Watson will destroy the cottage with your roughhousing."

Rose approached. "Did the police take Lois away?"

"Yes, and she left Reynard with me."

"You have a cat," Rose said.

I used to, Faith thought with a lump in her throat. Once again, she wondered where Watson had gone. This was absurd. He would be waiting for her outside the cottage tonight. He hadn't been home for dinner, and he never missed a meal if he could help it.

"Let me take Lois's dog," Rose offered. "I'll watch him until she returns. You look like you need to sit down."

"Thank you." Faith gratefully relinquished control of Reynard to the retreat director.

Marlene announced that the evening program had concluded and the police needed to sort out what had happened. She ushered people out of the room.

Wolfe took Faith's hand. "May I walk you and your parents to your cottage?"

She nodded, feeling safer with his nearness. "Thank you. I would like that."

They collected her parents and headed across the grounds to the gardener's cottage.

While her mother chattered nervously about Hannah's collapse, her father was silent. He might have been as anxious as Faith to review the clues they had compiled in their notebooks. Did this attempt on Hannah's life change their suspect list?

When they reached the front door, Watson was nowhere in sight. He rarely stayed out late, and it was well past ten o'clock. She thought of Watson's secret ways of accessing the cottage. He had to be waiting inside, upset that his dinner was late.

She unlocked the door and called for him several times.

When Watson didn't appear, they all spent nearly an hour searching every nook and cranny in the cottage and the flower beds and lawn outside.

The cat was missing.

Faith clutched her stomach, where the cupcake she had eaten earlier felt like it had turned to stone. Where could he be?

"I'm sure Watson will come back soon," her dad said. "He's only been gone for a few hours. Cats have a way of wandering off, then reappearing when you've given up on them."

While her mother was avidly involved in animal rescue, often fostering cats and dogs until good homes could be found for them, her father was not as emotionally attached to animals.

"You were right," Faith told her mother. "Watson has been feeling neglected. If I had paid more attention to him, he wouldn't have run away." She couldn't stop her tears.

Wolfe put his arms around her and held her close.

The warmth and comfort of his embrace eased some of her sorrow. Faith leaned back, gazed into Wolfe's blue eyes, and realized her parents had tactfully stepped into the kitchen. "You must think I'm silly, getting all weepy when my cat hasn't been gone a day."

"He's a resourceful fellow," Wolfe said. "But I understand your concern. It's not like him to disappear for long. He might be on the third floor of the manor. I'll do a thorough search for him when I get back there and let you know."

After Wolfe left, her mother called her into the kitchen for a cup of herbal tea. "This will settle your nerves."

Fresh tears streaked her cheeks. Faith wiped them away with a napkin. "I have this terrible feeling—"

Faith's cell phone buzzed with an incoming text message.

She checked the screen. "It's Wolfe. He says Watson isn't there but he's sure we'll find him in the morning. He's gone!"

Mom put her arm around Faith's shoulders. "He might be with Betsy. She didn't come to the play or the reception afterward. Watson could be in her room. But it's too late to check on that tonight."

Faith finally allowed her mother to coax her to bed, although she had a restless night without her warm, furry friend by her side.

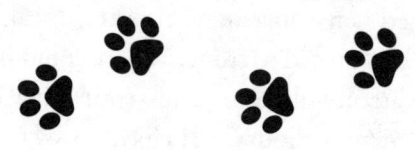

Thursday morning, Faith's parents prepared for an outing with Eileen to see the famous Freedom Trail, a walking tour of historical sites in Boston.

"I hate to miss a day of the retreat, but I so rarely get to spend time with my sister." Her mother reached across the kitchen table and placed her hand over Faith's, giving it a squeeze. "Are you sure you don't want to go with us?"

"I need to open the library. Besides, I want to be here if Watson—I mean, when—" Faith lifted her coffee cup to her mouth to hide her trembling lips, determined not to ruin her parents' vacation. "You'll love the Freedom Trail. Be sure to have lunch on the docks."

As soon as Eileen arrived, Faith told her that Watson was missing.

"I'm so sorry." Eileen hugged Faith. "But try not to worry. He'll come back soon."

Faith nodded, fighting tears.

Her parents walked into the room and greeted Eileen.

"Be sure to bring windbreakers and umbrellas," Eileen said. "There's a chance of precipitation this afternoon. We don't want to be caught on the Freedom Trail in a rainstorm." She glanced at her sister's stylish heeled sandals. "You might want different shoes. We're going to be walking several miles."

While her parents went to the guest room, Eileen touched Faith's arm. "I have some information for you."

Faith followed Eileen into the kitchen.

"Your mom told me she's proud of your dad for keeping out of the murder investigation, so forgive me for whispering."

"Too late. Dad's already in on it," Faith said. "He's even compiling case notes."

Eileen smiled. "Like father, like daughter."

"What did you find out?"

"I checked Lois's alibi. This will surprise you. I called the bookstore where she held her signing. Lois was there from four to sometime after six."

"That's what she said," Faith said, "but Lionel might have been killed before then."

"This is the interesting part," Eileen said. "The bookstore owner said Lois was a few minutes late. She volunteers at a library in a children's literacy program. She was at the program from two to four, then arrived at the book signing."

"Why wouldn't she tell people about the program?" Faith asked. "By not mentioning it, she made herself seem guilty."

"The bookstore owner told me Lois doesn't want people to think she's trying to gain attention for her novels through her volunteer work. That's quite admirable."

"If she really was at the library," Faith said. "What if Lois was late to her book signing because she was busy murdering Lionel?"

"That's possible. I haven't called the library to verify Lois was there." Eileen studied Faith for a moment. "I was under the impression you thought Lois is innocent. What changed?"

Faith quickly told her aunt about the poisoned lavender cookie and Hannah's implication that it was the same herb used in one of Lois's books. "I hope Lois let the police know about the literacy program. They seem to think she's the prime suspect."

Eileen stared at her. "What if someone is using a murder method from one of her novels in an effort to frame her?"

On her way to the manor that morning, Faith was startled to see Hannah enter the Victorian garden. Whatever had caused her collapse the previous night must not have been too serious. The redhead was pale, but apparently she felt well enough to attend the first session of the day.

Many guests were clearly excited about the talk regarding the secret history of the manor. The speaker had promised to reveal fascinating details about the grand estate, including some of the hidden passages.

Faith knew most of those things about the manor, so she decided to skip the talk. Instead, she called Brooke and Midge to tell them about Watson. She told everyone she met that her black-and-white cat with a stubby tail was missing and asked them to watch for him. She knew she must be a mess, her eyes puffy from crying the night before and her lips trembling.

She scanned the lawn and gardens as she walked. When she glimpsed a tail disappearing into a hedge, her heart jumped. But the tail was long, bushy, and gray. Wrong length, wrong texture, wrong color. It belonged to a squirrel.

At the library, Faith kept imagining she spied Watson from the corner of her eye. She tried to focus on the patrons, many of whom sought hints for the location of the fourth hidden treasure.

"What was the quote?" Faith asked one of the guests.

"I'll read it to you." The slender young man scrolled through his tablet. "'It was like a king's canopy, a fairy king's. There were flowering cherry-trees near and apple-trees whose buds were pink and white, and here and there one had burst open wide. Between the blossoming branches of the canopy bits of blue sky looked down like wonderful eyes.'"

"As a staff member, I can't give hints," Faith said. "But think about what the author described."

"It sounds like an orchard." The young man slipped the tablet into his retreat tote bag. "Is there an orchard at the manor?"

"Check your map," Faith told him.

A guest standing behind the young man whispered to her companion, "Orchard." Then both headed out of the library.

The young man hurried after them.

Faith struggled to be attentive and professional, but her thoughts kept returning to her missing cat. On her break, she raced up to the third floor. Charlotte helped her search for Watson, but he wasn't sunning in a window or sleeping on a favorite pillow.

Dejected, Faith returned to the library. Her nerves were thoroughly frayed by the time she called Betsy's room. There was no answer. She left a message, realizing she probably sounded hysterical.

An hour later, Betsy rolled into the library in her red wheelchair. "I came as soon as I heard your message. Have you found your sweet kitty yet?"

"No," Faith said. "I was hoping he was with you."

"I haven't seen Mr. Watson since Wednesday morning," Betsy said. "I've been watching for him. He likes riding with me."

They reviewed Watson's comings and goings during the past day.

"And you didn't see him after that dog chased him into the elevator?" Betsy asked.

"Mrs. Jaxon reported he came upstairs with her," Faith said. "Nobody has seen him since."

Faith's cell phone rang. It was Midge.

"Has Watson reappeared yet?" Midge asked without preamble.

"No," Faith answered. "I have no idea where he could be."

"I'm sure he'll return soon. That cat of yours is resourceful. But I've called about another pet. I'm afraid I have some bad news."

"Oh no. What is it?" Faith asked with no small amount of trepidation. She wasn't sure she could take another animal-related tragedy at the moment.

"I reached Lionel's sons and his sister. They can't take Patches. They're the only family members I know of to call. This puppy needs a foster home. He's going to get depressed if he stays in my clinic kennel much longer, even though we've all been loving on him every chance we get."

Faith nearly said she would take the Pomeranian. After all, she was bereft of her cat. *Temporarily*, Faith reminded herself. Watson would come home soon. She glanced at Betsy. "I have an idea about Patches," she told Midge. "I'll call you back."

"Okay. You be strong. And let me know as soon as Watson returns."

After she hung up, Faith said to Betsy, "You mentioned that Watson was helping to heal your heart. And he made you realize you might be ready for another animal companion."

"Yes," Betsy said cautiously. "I have to admit your cat has won my heart. But I'm really a dog person."

"I know of a puppy in need of a home. Lionel's Pomeranian, Patches."

Betsy pressed a hand to her mouth, as if not trusting herself to speak. After a moment, she lowered her hand. "This is rather sudden. I need to think about it."

"Of course. Patches is being cared for at Dr. Midge Foster's clinic. They're giving him all the love and attention they can, but he'll need a home soon."

"Yes, he will," Betsy said, then abruptly turned and wheeled out of the library.

As much as Midge wanted Patches placed in a forever home, Betsy might not be ready for a new companion yet after all. Faith knew too well how attached a person could be to her pet. Betsy might want another Maltese, like her previous dog. If Betsy didn't take Patches, perhaps Faith's mother could give him a temporary home. She would ask if Betsy said no.

Faith's thoughts quickly returned to Watson, a cat who had a home. If she couldn't push her debilitating worry from her mind, she might as well quit work for the day. But she would have less to distract her in the cottage. Besides, Watson could stroll into the library at any moment. She needed to stay. He would show up today. He had to.

The only way she could stop fretting over her missing cat was to focus on solving the murder.

14

Faith noted the information Eileen had given her about Lois's volunteer work in her notebook. If it checked out as true, Lois had a solid alibi. *If.* But that still left three suspects.

Perhaps an employee had become upset enough to kill the famous gardener. Damian had had time to commit the murder after returning from the hospital.

Jeremiah had stepped out of Lionel's shadow to give the speech Monday night. The forest gardener had been eager to volunteer, and he was remarkably prepared. Had he bumped off his competition in the world of gardening so his own light could shine brighter?

Hannah had a personal grudge against Lionel. She blamed him for spraying chemicals, causing her to lose her organic license for two years. Yet she had been poisoned last night, so wasn't she more likely a victim than a criminal?

Faith called Glenn, hoping to check out Hannah's alibi about getting a ride to her farm Monday. She got the same message from his voice mail. He was still fishing.

As Faith mulled over the clues and alibis, she kept coming back to the evidence. Hannah had claimed the cookie she'd been eating was poisoned with an herb from Lois's fourth book in her gardening series.

Faith went to the bookcase housing mysteries. She found the book Hannah had referenced.

The title was *The Long Kiss Good Nightshade.*

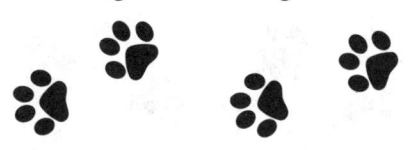

The cat dozed fitfully. His kind were known to sleep frequently, requiring rest between forays of feather-toy attacks and mouse hunting, but sleep was no cure for his present situation. He tried to stand and stretch. The confines of the box allowed precious little movement.

The darkness was complete and terrifying. He shuddered. The last time he had felt this alone was when he had been abandoned in the city as a kitten. If not for his human rescuing him from the streets, he might not be alive today. And today might be the sum total of his remaining existence if he didn't escape soon. Where was his human?

The musty odor offended his sensitive nose. He clawed at the side of the box, shredding cloth with his sharp claws and exposing a narrow gap between the boards. Precious fresh air filled his lungs, and a faint glimmer of light seeped in.

The whirring, thumping, tumbling noise of a machine distracted him. Someone was in the other room. Once before, he had observed the nice lady throwing items into one machine to get them wet, then placing them in the warming machine to dry them. Even though every cat knew a sandpapery tongue was the best cleaning method.

The warmth of linens fresh from the machine was what had led to his discovery of the hole in the wall and the hidden room. He couldn't believe he had allowed himself to be lured to his doom so easily.

He focused on the sound. Beneath the rumbling he heard footsteps. He meowed loudly.

"Hello?" It was the nice lady with the new feather toy. "Is somebody there?"

He howled at the top of his lungs.

Rushing water drowned out his plaintive cries as the wet machine filled. The nice lady couldn't hear him over the racket of the machine.

He curled into a tight ball, miserable with hunger and fear.

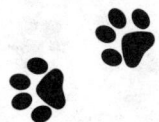

When Lois entered the library, Faith hoped she could engage the author in a conversation that might reveal clues to Lionel's death.

Instead, Lois hurried to Faith's desk. "My discussion panel about red herrings in gardening mysteries starts in ten minutes. Reynard can't sit still through two talks in a row." She handed Faith the dog's leash. "I hope you don't mind watching him. I'll be back right after the discussion."

Before Faith could object, Lois spun around and was gone.

Reynard gazed up at Faith, a silly doggy smile exposing sharp teeth and a pink tongue. His curled tail wagged.

"I guess we're stuck with each other for the next hour," Faith told the dog.

Guests suddenly seemed to find any excuse to come to Faith's desk to ask questions. All patted the unique-looking dog.

Reynard soaked up the attention.

When the next discussion started, the library emptied, except for a gentleman sitting in front of the bouquet-filled fireplace, reading a newspaper.

"Faith, do you need any help?" Laura scratched Reynard behind the ears. "I'm on break, and I need to work on a school project."

Faith briefly considered asking Laura to walk the dog, then decided the college student would benefit more from experience in the library. Besides, it was a beautiful summer day, and Faith was weary of moping around, worrying about Watson.

"That would be great. I'm watching Reynard until Ms. Girten comes back. He would probably rather go for a walk than sit in the library."

Reynard seemed to know what the word *walk* meant. He sprang to his feet and gazed at her hopefully.

Faith guided him to the French doors and then outside.

Reynard tugged on the leash, anxious to explore a stand of white oak trees. Natural wooded areas dotted the grounds, places where squirrels and other woodland creatures could find sanctuary from predators like Reynard. Walking paths and benches encouraged guests to enjoy the patches of untamed forest along the edges of the immaculately groomed lawns and gardens.

Faith struggled to keep up as Reynard frolicked at the end of the leash, snapping at butterflies. Suddenly he headed toward the trees again, determined to drag Faith with him.

She glimpsed a flutter of brown wings, then a patch of navy blue. Sunlight illuminated Jeremiah and Sage for a moment. Faith entered on a path, surprised by the dramatic temperature drop in the shade of the trees. Lush green foliage shielded the interior of the miniature forest from the August sun. The woods felt remote and secluded. Maybe too secluded to be following a potential murder suspect.

The gardener sat on the ground beneath an oak tree that must have been at least a hundred years old, judging by its girth and height. The owl hopped along a low branch, flapping one wing while the other remained tucked against his side.

As she approached, Jeremiah continued studying a small, battered book in his lap.

Faith realized it was a Bible. Concerned she had interrupted his meditation, she tried to back away quietly.

Reynard jerked on the leash and barked at the small owl.

Jeremiah glanced up.

"I'm sorry to disturb you," Faith said. "I'm letting Reynard burn off some energy."

The gardener pulled an old-fashioned timepiece from one of the many voluminous pockets on his cargo shorts. "I completely lost track of time." He returned the watch to his pocket, then stood slowly and stretched. "I needed a few minutes of quiet. I'm not used to being around crowds. It's sort of draining."

"I know what you mean," Faith said. "Sometimes all I want is to be alone with a good book."

"Or *the* Good Book." Jeremiah smiled. "You're a librarian, right?

A roomful of books must be your sanctuary." He waved an arm around. "The woods are a sanctuary to me. I find peace of mind here."

Faith felt guilty about her intention to question Jeremiah. He was reading the Bible. He couldn't be a murderer. Then she thought of the shocking cases of murder and mayhem with a supposedly religious person at the epicenter. The woodsy gardener either needed to be cleared of suspicion or verified as the culprit.

"You seemed right at home when you spoke to an audience Monday night," Faith said. "And you've done a great job on your panel discussions."

"That's different. I love talking to people about gardening and nature. It's being crowded into small spaces with dozens of strangers that wears me down."

"I can understand that." Faith couldn't think of anywhere in the manor that qualified as a small space, but she supposed that any building might feel small to a man who was used to being outside. "Louis Pasteur said, 'Fortune favors the prepared mind.' You must have been thrilled to have the sudden opportunity to speak in Lionel's place."

"Yes, that was unexpected. I gained a lot of subscribers to my gardening blog that evening. To think, while I was speaking, Lionel was—well, it's a sad deal." Jeremiah called to the owl.

Sage fluttered awkwardly out of the tree to perch on his outstretched arm.

Reynard danced on his hind legs.

"I think this dog is eager to greet you," Jeremiah told Sage, then lowered his arm.

Reynard touched his nose to the bird's shiny beak and wagged his tail.

Sage's feathers fluffed, making him appear twice his size, then smoothed back down. Apparently he'd made his point.

Jeremiah turned to Faith. "I stopped by the library yesterday afternoon for the book I ordered from the shop in Boston, but I didn't see it."

"I tucked it inside my desk to keep it safe," Faith explained. "I didn't feel comfortable leaving the book sitting out. But I told Laura you were going to pick it up."

"Laura was mobbed by guests, and I had to get to a talk."

Faith remembered rescuing Laura from five aggressive people clamoring for answers to their many questions. "Then the book is still in the drawer."

"I hope so," Jeremiah said. "It wasn't cheap."

"The library is locked when no one is there to watch it," Faith assured him.

"Well, I can't wait to see it. From references to the book I've read in other sources, it documents native medicinal herbs." Jeremiah scanned the area. "This patch of forest may have been undisturbed since Colonial times. There's a chance some rare old plants are growing here."

"Really?"

Jeremiah touched his boot to a piece of disturbed earth. "It looks like someone picked a bunch of this plant and wasn't gentle about it."

"What kind of plant is it?" Faith asked.

He crouched down, examining the plant without touching it. "It's not exactly the same plant I know in the Maine woods, but it could be poisonous."

Faith gasped. "Poisonous? What if it's the herb that made Hannah sick last night?" She snapped her mouth shut. That probably wasn't a good thing to say if Jeremiah was the person who had poisoned her and possibly killed Lionel too. But if he was guilty, he wouldn't point out the herb. Would he?

"I'll come back with the book later. Hopefully it will help me make a definite identification." Jeremiah consulted his timepiece again. "Time to go," he said with a little sigh.

"I need to return Reynard to Lois," Faith said. "I'll walk with you. If you have a moment, I'll get your book."

As they neared the manor, Faith nearly asked where he had been at the time of Lionel's demise, but she managed to hold her tongue.

Fortunately, Jeremiah saved her the task of an amateur interrogation. "The police interviewed me. I suppose they questioned a lot of guests, but I felt like they suspected me."

"The Lighthouse Bay police are thorough and fair," Faith said.

Sage wobbled on Jeremiah's shoulder.

He reached up and stroked the owl's feathers. "I don't think they liked my answer. I wasn't ready for the retreat crowd. Mostly I'm in the woods alone or in my remote cabin. My interactions with humans are usually via the Internet. Face-to-face communication is a whole different deal."

"That's true," Faith said.

Jeremiah's face twisted in a rueful smile. "I'm really introverted. Being on a subway or in a roomful of strangers almost throws me into a panic attack. So during my first break at the retreat, I snuck off to this patch of trees to collect my thoughts. I was gone during the time Lionel—well, I hope they find the real killer, or they might try to pin it on me."

"I'm sure the police will learn the truth soon," Faith said as they reached the manor.

"Thanks for listening," Jeremiah said. "I've been worried sick, thinking there might be a murderer at the retreat laughing at us dupes while plotting to kill someone else. If they haven't already struck."

"What do you mean?" Faith asked.

"Last night. Hannah and the poisoned cookie. Who knows what'll happen next?"

As they approached the loggia, a group of guests surrounded the black-haired young man who had been asking Faith for hints to the hidden treasure earlier. Spread on a table were books and jars.

"I found it in the orchard." The young man's dark eyes shone with excitement. "There are fruit jams and jellies from the manor's orchard and berry patch." He held up one jar filled with rich purple preserves, then set it on the table and lifted a book. "Also, books on growing fruit trees and bushes. And even a gift certificate to a nursery specializing in plants for home gardeners."

Faith thought hiding gifts had been a terrific idea. Guests were encouraged to read *The Secret Garden* and explore the impressive grounds.

Lois stepped around the group admiring the treasure and approached Faith and Jeremiah. "Thank you for watching Reynard," she told Faith as she took her dog's leash. "I hope he wasn't too much trouble."

"He was a perfect gentleman," Faith said. "It was no problem. I took him for a walk to a patch of forest on the grounds." She watched Lois's face for any reaction indicating she had prowled around those same woods seeking poisonous herbs.

"Maybe Reynard will behave himself for the rest of the day," Lois said.

When Lois left, Faith and Jeremiah made it to the library with no more interruptions.

Laura sat at the table, scribbling notes in a three-ring binder as she read a textbook. "Did Reynard have a nice walk?"

"I'm not sure the walk had much effect on his energy level," Faith said as she moved behind the desk and opened the deep drawer. She frowned. Jeremiah's book wasn't there. "Laura, did you move the package?"

"No." Laura's already pale complexion went a shade lighter as the blood seemed to drain from her face. She rushed over and peered into the empty drawer. "It's not there?"

After a series of questions that sent Laura to the brink of tears, both Faith and Jeremiah decided the book had been removed from the desk Wednesday afternoon while library patrons had distracted the young woman. Anyone could have taken the book when Laura was hemmed in at the bookcases.

"I feel terrible," Laura said. "I'll pay for the book. If it was lost while I was on duty, it's my responsibility."

Faith knew the college student didn't have money to spare. Laura had made the offer sincerely, but she would be devastated when she learned how much the book had cost.

"We need to be sure the book is actually gone first." Faith turned to Jeremiah. "Laura and I will do a thorough search of the library."

"I could let all the housekeeping staff know to watch for the book in the guest rooms," Laura suggested. "In case someone accidentally took the book to his or her room."

"Good idea," Faith said.

"If someone took the book by mistake, I'm sure they'll return it soon," Jeremiah said.

Faith was not as confident. The package could not have been removed from the desk by mistake. That would have required snooping and taking something that clearly belonged to someone else.

The book had been stolen.

15

Jeremiah took the news that his book was missing remarkably well, considering that he had searched for it for years and it was monetarily as well as historically valuable.

Faith sent Jeremiah to Marlene's basement office to report his stolen book. Marlene would not be happy to deal with another guest issue, but she would know how to handle the situation.

That afternoon, most guests attended the screening of a British mystery show with a gardening theme. Faith and Laura took advantage of the quiet to search the library for Jeremiah's book. It was a daunting task, considering thousands of old volumes lined the two stories of bookshelves.

Their efforts ended in disappointment, and Faith gave Laura more assurances that she hadn't done anything wrong.

At three, Laura left to attend a college class.

When she was gone, Faith pulled out her notebook and jotted down notes about her conversation with Jeremiah. She added the mysteriously missing book that just happened to contain a chapter on local poisonous plants. Then there was the matter of the disturbed plant in the patch of old white oaks too. Had Jeremiah faked the theft of the book to cover up his use of it to poison Hannah?

Faith was sick at heart when she thought of how easy it would have been for her to place the book in the manor safe. She reminded herself that hindsight was twenty-twenty.

When Faith was finished writing, she called Midge.

"Have you found Watson yet?" Midge asked immediately.

"I'm afraid not." Faith tried to keep her voice steady. "But I've been so busy with the retreat that I haven't had much time to search."

"I know he'll turn up," Midge said soothingly. "It's not like Watson to disappear for long. He's probably exploring or maybe hanging out with Betsy."

"That's actually why I called," Faith said. "Betsy didn't have Watson with her. But I told Betsy that Patches might be available for adoption, and she sounded interested but a little hesitant. I'm not sure she's ready for a new dog quite yet."

"There's an easy way to find out. I'll bring Patches to the manor after I close the clinic today. I know she'll fall in love with him. Everyone at the clinic has."

"I wish I could see her reaction," Faith said. "But I'm going to dinner with my parents and Jenna's family tonight."

"Well, I wouldn't sound disappointed about that," Midge said. "Dinner with your entire family is a real treat."

"I know," Faith said. "But I'm worried that Watson could come home while we're out. He might feel abandoned."

"Watson is a resourceful cat," Midge answered. "Remember, he has secret ways in and out of your cottage. I'm sure he's fine. What about you, though? Are you okay?"

Faith assured her friend that she was coping with what she hoped was Watson's temporary disappearance. In reality, she was beginning to feel frantic. *Where is that cat?*

After she hung up the phone, Faith tried to keep busy. But the remaining hours of the afternoon stretched too long.

Finally, it was time to lock up the library. On her walk to the gardener's cottage, she watched for Watson, but she didn't see any sign of him.

Eileen's car was parked at the house, which meant her parents were back from their day in Boston. Maybe they had let Watson inside already.

Faith threw open the door, hoping to see her cat. She rushed inside, glanced around the living area, then peeked into the kitchen.

Her father and mother sat at the table, and her aunt poured steaming water from a teakettle into three cups.

Faith spun around and raced to her bedroom.

"Where's the fire?" her dad called.

"The reservation isn't until six thirty," her mom added. "You have time for a cup of tea."

Faith surveyed the room, opening closet doors and peering behind curtains and under her bed. After several minutes of fruitless searching, she clumped slowly into the kitchen. "I was hoping Watson would be home."

"We just arrived a few minutes ago," her mom said. "He wasn't here."

Eileen returned the kettle to the stove. "The manor grounds offer opportunity for all sorts of exploration, and Watson is a curious cat. I'm sure he'll show up after he has thoroughly investigated whatever has caught his attention."

Faith tried to banish the phrase that entered her head. *Curiosity killed the cat.*

"Are you sure you won't go to dinner with us?" Mom asked Eileen. "It will only be the Newberry clan tonight."

"I'd love to, but it's been a long day," Eileen said. "I'm afraid I've already pushed myself to the limit."

Eileen had rheumatoid arthritis and had to be careful not to overdo it. Walking the Freedom Trail in the heat and humidity surely qualified as overdoing it.

Faith poured herself a cup of tea and sat at the table, trying to focus on the conversation.

They were thankful they'd taken umbrellas, as a brief rain shower had caught them as they crossed a park, with no opportunity to run for shelter. Her father was glad when the walking tour took them to Paul Revere's home. Her mother enjoyed seeing the Old North Church and marveled at the simple yet beautiful architecture.

But they seemed to realize Faith's mind was elsewhere, and the tale faded away until it was time to leave for dinner.

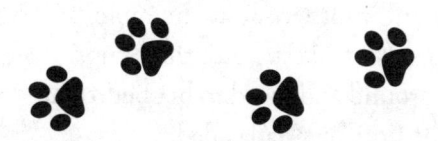

Later that evening at the small seafood restaurant in a nearby village, Faith tried to concentrate on the delicious dinner and chatting with Jenna and her husband, Nick. Faith's nephew, Oliver, was in his usual high spirits and had many stories to tell them about school, but even his antics couldn't get Faith's mind off her missing cat. She did her best to put on a brave face.

When they arrived back at Faith's cottage, she was glad she had eaten so little. Her stomach churned with anxiety when Watson wasn't waiting for them. This should be the happiest time of her life. Her wedding was weeks away, her family was in good health, and she had the best job she could imagine. Without Watson, though, she was miserable.

In the wee hours of the night, Faith gave up. Her furry companion's absence made sleep impossible. She took her notebook out of her bag and tiptoed to the kitchen. The light was on. Faith's heart thudded as she crept to the doorway and peeked in.

Her father sat with his notebook open on the table.

"Great minds think alike," Faith said, raising her notebook.

He glanced up, clearly startled. Then he smiled and patted the seat next to him. "Couldn't sleep," he said softly. "Rather than wake your mother with my tossing and turning, I decided to review my notes."

"I can't sleep either." Faith's eyes filled with tears. "Watson—"

He put an arm around her. "It'll be okay. How about we try something your mother would recommend? A little prayer."

"I should have thought of that earlier," Faith said.

They clasped hands, and her father prayed. "Please allow the little cat who has captured my daughter's heart to be returned safely and soon. Amen."

It reminded Faith of all the times he'd prayed away nightmares when she was a little girl, and the simple action soothed her.

Faith stood. "Hot cocoa?" she asked.

"Absolutely."

In a few minutes, Faith set two mugs of cocoa on the table. Then they started reviewing case notes. Faith told her father about Jeremiah's missing book, with its chapter on indigenous poisonous herbs, and the disturbed mound of plants in the woods near where Jeremiah had been reading his Bible.

"Hannah became ill, but she didn't die," her dad said. "That might indicate an incompetent murderer, or Hannah could be paranoid. Maybe she imagined someone tried to poison her when it was a simple case of fainting on a warm summer night." He tapped a pencil on the open page of his notebook. "Motivation. Who would want Hannah dead?"

"Jeremiah might have 'stolen' his own book to throw the police off after he used it to find a poisonous plant. But I don't know why he would want to kill Hannah." Faith rested her elbows on the table and her forehead in her hand. "How did you manage to solve all those crimes? There are so many clues and suspects."

"Careful police work." Her father lifted his mug of hot cocoa and took a sip. "It's not like on the television shows, where crimes are solved in an hour, with commercials. Often it can take a considerable amount of time."

"We don't have much time," Faith reminded him. "The retreat ends the day after tomorrow. When all the guests leave, won't it be more difficult to solve Lionel's murder?"

"True." He flipped to a new page in his notebook. "So we'd better see this thing through."

Sitting up with her father did not make sleep come any easier for Faith when she finally went to bed.

Still, she managed to doze for a few fitful hours before her alarm sounded Friday morning. Faith crawled out of bed, heartsick that Watson had not materialized during the night.

She sent a text to Wolfe. *Watson is still missing. Have you seen him upstairs?*

Wolfe replied immediately. *We searched everywhere. Mother will keep looking, and she has the staff watching for him too. I have to work in Boston today, but I'll help search again tonight if necessary. I'm sure he'll be found before then.*

Faith sighed. Maybe it would help if she spread the word about Watson's disappearance, so she called Rose and asked her to inform the guests.

After Faith showered and got ready, she and her parents went to the buffet in the manor's sunny breakfast room.

Rose stood at the podium and announced that Watson was missing. She requested that guests be on the lookout for a stubby-tailed black-and-white cat.

Next, Rose announced the fifth hidden treasure clue. "In *The Secret Garden*, Mary says to Colin, 'Everything is a kind of secret. Rooms are locked up and gardens are locked up—and you! Have you been locked up?' This might be one of the more difficult clues, but we have confidence our Hidden Treasures Literary and Gardening Retreat guests are clever and resourceful. You've found four treasures so far. Good luck with number five."

Faith left most of her breakfast on her plate. She excused herself from the table. "I open the library in half an hour," she explained to her parents. "I have time to search for Watson. Maybe he's trapped in one of the hidden passageways."

Dad placed his napkin on the table. "I'll go with you."

It was comforting having her father accompany her in the search for Watson. Faith might have enjoyed showing him the secrets hidden inside the old manor if their quest had not been so serious. Thirty minutes flew by too swiftly. Watson was not in any of his usual hiding places.

"I'll keep snooping around," her father said. "Try not to worry. Watson will turn up."

Faith was glad that guests kept her busy that morning. She had little time to fret about Watson.

Just before noon, her desk phone chimed. As it had every time since Watson disappeared, her heart jumped at the sound and the potential for news about her cat.

"Can you take a break for lunch?" Brooke asked. "I've already prepared the food for the picnic for the guests, so I'm free."

"I was planning to close the library during my break," Faith said. "I should use the time to search for Watson."

"I have some updates to share. And some treats."

Faith realized she hadn't eaten much during the past twenty-four hours. She suddenly felt light-headed from lack of food as much as from worry. "I do need to eat something. I'll meet you in the lobby in five minutes."

The library emptied as excited guests headed for the Victorian garden and the promise of an old-fashioned picnic with a modern flair.

Faith locked the door and met Brooke in the lobby. They strolled to a secluded bench near the Peter Pan fountain. Water splashed, providing soothing background noise to Brooke's revelations.

"First, you have to try this egg salad," Brooke said. "It's seasoned with herbs from the garden."

Egg salad could be a bland sandwich filling, but Brooke's version was subtly flavorful and encased in a flaky, buttery croissant. "It's delicious. Is your news as good?"

"I'm happy to say the kitchen staff, myself included, has been cleared of either purposefully or accidentally putting the poisonous plant in Hannah's dessert the other night."

"That's great," Faith said. "Not that I thought for a minute that you or your staff was responsible."

"Officer Laddy let slip a tidbit of info." Brooke's face flushed, as it often did when she spoke about the handsome young policeman.

"What did he tell you?"

"They took samples of the rest of the desserts, but there was no poison found in anything except Hannah's cookie," Brooke replied. "Also, Lois used the same plant in one of her murder mysteries, but she couldn't identify it from photos the police had."

"Unless she was lying," Faith said. "She has to know that identifying the plant would make her a suspect in Hannah's poisoning."

"Laddy wouldn't tell me all the details, but he did say they searched Lois's tote bag again, which did not make her happy. There was no trace of the herb on her, in the bag, or in her room."

"They were certainly thorough. Did they search any other guests?"

"I'm not sure," Brooke answered. "Laddy wouldn't tell me."

"Eileen said Lois might be accounted for during the time of the murder." Faith described the author's secretive volunteer work at a children's literacy program in a library, followed closely by the book signing. "If that's true, we can count her out as a suspect. Eileen needs to verify her alibi, though. Most of the evidence still points to Lois."

"For both Lionel's murder and Hannah's poisoning."

Faith nodded. "We have to keep in mind that half the retreat guests probably know enough about herbs to have poisoned Hannah. Especially the people speaking on panels or giving demonstrations. That includes Damian and Hannah, but I think we can cross Jeremiah's name off the suspect list."

"Why do you say that?"

Faith caught Brooke up to speed on her concerns about Jeremiah's potential motivation—eliminating his celebrity competition and bringing attention to himself. She told Brooke about her conversation with the gardener in the patch of woods.

"I don't know. It seems like you're letting him off the hook just because he was reading the Bible. He might have made it look like his book was stolen to cover up making the poison that sent Hannah to the emergency room."

"But why? Unless Hannah knew Jeremiah is the killer. But both Lois and Hannah have stronger motivations to want Lionel dead. Even Damian might have been angry with his employer for reasons we don't yet know. Damian certainly knows enough about herbs to poison someone. Did Laddy let slip any information about him?"

"I was lucky to hear as much as I did," Brooke said. "The retreat ends tomorrow. We're running out of time. What are we going to do?"

"Your guess is as good as mine. I don't think we're any closer to solving this than when we started."

16

The cat sneezed. As his tummy rumbled with painful hunger pangs, he feared he wouldn't survive much longer.

Then he heard voices. The nice lady was back.

"Here's the hole," the nice lady said. "That's funny. The cardboard I placed there has been moved."

"Mice," a man's voice said. "They can be determined little things."

"Then it's even more imperative this is fixed as quickly as possible. I realize it's only a linen closet, but it's important to maintain the historical integrity of every square inch of the manor. Do you think you can restore the wall to its original condition?"

"Yes, but I'll have to remove the shelving to do the repair. You won't even be able to tell there was a hole in the wall when I'm done. After I make a trip to the hardware store, I can start right away."

"Wonderful! I found dust and cobwebs on my clean towels. I hate to think what might be living inside that wall."

The cat had given up all hope that the nice lady could hear his mewing. Still, it might be his last chance to be found. As old as the wood-and-leather box smelled, he might never be found, even after he was mere bones and fur.

All of his anguish and fear welled up into a single yowl, the loudest he had ever released.

"What was that?" the man asked.

"It came from inside the wall," the nice lady said. "Can you see anything?"

The cat inhaled a deep breath but choked on dust. He sneezed instead.

"Dark as a cave," the man said. "More than likely, it's only the old house creaking and settling."

The footsteps of humans moving away nearly shattered the cat's last shred of hope, but he refused to give up. He attempted a last howl.

"*I know that voice,*" the nice lady said.

The cat heard scraping sounds.

"*You're making it worse, Mrs. Jaxon.*"

"*We've been turning the manor upside down searching for a small black-and-white cat. What if that's him?*"

"*Wait,*" the man said. "*Let me get my toolbox.*"

The cat clawed at the lid of the box, desperate to escape and not trusting the humans to reach him in time.

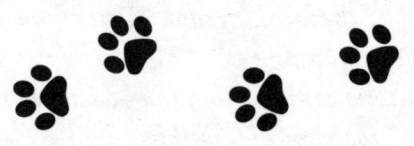

Brooke's information added to what Faith knew about the suspects in Lionel's murder, but she was far from figuring out who the killer was.

Faith's cell phone chimed, barely audible over the splashing water in the Peter Pan fountain. She glanced at the caller ID. "It's Charlotte," she told Brooke before she answered.

"We found Watson." Charlotte sounded as though she had been running. She sneezed.

"Is he okay?" Faith's stomach lurched, afraid of the answer.

A male voice in the background asked a question Faith couldn't quite hear.

"Yes, as quickly as you can," Charlotte said to him. She paused a beat as a loud hammering sound began, then said to Faith, "Come upstairs right away, and bring your parents if you can find them. You all need to see this." She hung up before Faith could ask any more questions.

"You look pale," Brooke said. "What happened?"

"I don't know," Faith admitted. "Charlotte told me to get my parents and hurry upstairs. She found Watson."

"That's good, right?" Brooke asked.

"I hope so, but she didn't really say."

"I have to get back to the kitchen." Brooke gave Faith's hand a quick squeeze, then started to clean up from their picnic. "Call if you need me."

Faith sprinted toward the nearest manor entrance. Fortunately, Faith's parents were exiting the salon. She grabbed her mother's arm and gave a breathless explanation. They were in too much of a hurry to wait for the elevator, so they ran up the stairs.

Faith burst into the living room. Charlotte knelt on the floor, stroking a familiar if dusty furry figure as the cat gulped food from a dish. Even from across the room, Faith could hear his purring.

"Watson!" Faith cried as she hurried across the room.

Watson whipped around to face her, his green eyes wide with excitement. He launched himself into Faith's arms.

"Oh, Watson! I was so worried. Are you okay?" She held the stubby-tailed cat at arm's length and checked him over.

"He was definitely hungry," Charlotte said. "He's on his second can of food I had on hand for him in case we found him."

"Where was he?" Dad asked.

"I'll show you. Come with me." Charlotte stood and led them down a hallway. "We very nearly sealed Watson inside a hidden room permanently."

Faith followed Charlotte down a corridor, through the laundry room, and into a linen closet. A human-size hole had been carved out of the plaster wall between two framing studs.

Charlotte slipped through. "Come on in," she said.

Her father squeezed his large frame through the narrow opening.

As Faith stepped near, Watson dug his claws into her shoulder and shuddered. "I'll wait out here," she said. "Watson doesn't want anything to do with this."

"I'll hold him," her mother offered.

Faith reluctantly handed Watson to her mom. He mewed a sharp warning when Faith stepped through the hole in the wall.

"What is this?" Faith whispered.

"I don't understand," her dad said, glancing around. "What's so important that we had to rush up here?"

"Watson discovered an old sea chest." Charlotte lowered the domed lid and aimed a flashlight at elegant script carved with the name *J. Newberry*. "My guess is that it belonged to Josiah Newberry."

"That's odd," Mom called. "Why would a Newberry chest be hidden in the manor?"

Faith cringed. Her father had struggled to accept that the Jaxon family had not wronged the Newberry family generations ago. Now, despite that evidence, here was a sea chest that had been walled away in the manor.

Dad lifted the lid and stared into the jumbled sea chest. "I don't understand," he repeated.

"Watson was inside the chest," Charlotte said. "A repairman and I heard him yowling while we discussed fixing the hole in the wall permanently. Watson must have crawled inside and gotten trapped."

Faith stopped her father from reaching into the trunk. "Hold on. Everything in there is probably fragile." Her training as an archivist kicked in. "Charlotte, do you have gloves? Any kind will do, as long as they're clean."

Charlotte slipped out of the room and returned a minute later with a pair of disposable nitrile gloves.

After Faith's father pulled on the gloves, stretched tight over his large hands, he hesitated.

Faith touched his arm. "What's wrong?"

"I'm afraid it will all crumble to dust. We have so little from my side of the family. This is a connection to my family." His voice caught in his throat. "Our history."

"Maybe we should contact Lou Bennett from the Lighthouse Bay Whaling Museum," Faith suggested.

"Excellent idea," Charlotte said. "I'll call him."

Faith and Charlotte stepped out of the secret room.

Faith took Watson from her mother, then smiled at Charlotte. "I can't thank you enough." She couldn't stop the tears from spilling down her cheeks.

Charlotte's eyes filled with tears too. "I've come to think of him as my grandcat. I'm just thankful Watson let us know where he was before it was too late."

Too late. That was what frightened Faith. Watson trembled as he glanced back at the hole in the wall. Faith held him tight.

"He's an independent soul," her father called from the hidden room. "That cat will only stand for so much coddling."

"Still, we should take Watson to the cottage." Mom touched Faith's arm. "He could use a good grooming. It will settle his nerves to get away from the prison where he spent the last two nights."

"I'll stay here," her father said. "I want to hear what Mr. Bennett has to say before we try to move this." He tore his gaze from the sea chest. "I'm glad you located your cat. He's quite the detective, finding my family's hidden trunk. Although what it's doing here..."

"Don't look a gift horse in the mouth," her mother said. "Finding the chest is a blessing. And we owe it to Watson." She rubbed the cat's head. "Now let's get you home."

When the elevator neared the first floor, Watson wriggled in Faith's arms. He seemed to be recovering quickly, but Faith was not rebounding as fast. She still felt weak with relief that he had been found safe and sound. Faith set Watson on the floor of the elevator as the door opened.

When they stepped out onto the main floor, Betsy rolled toward them. "I see you have Watson back. How wonderful!"

"I'm so happy." Once again, tears of relief filled Faith's eyes. "He was stuck behind a wall. If Mrs. Jaxon hadn't heard him meowing—" Faith paused. "Well, he's back and he's safe."

"I'm so relieved, and I can only imagine how you must feel. I was actually coming to find you. I wanted to thank you for putting me in contact with Midge. She brought Patches to meet me last night."

"Did you like him?" Faith's mother asked.

"Oh yes, we hit it off right away," Betsy said. "I'm seriously considering adopting him, but it's difficult making a decision this important in a rush. I'm going to let Midge know tomorrow whether I'm taking Patches home with me."

"That's wise," Mom said. "I often foster homeless cats and dogs, and adoptions work better when people take their time to—"

A familiar woof interrupted Faith's mother. Reynard galloped toward them, trailing his leash across the tile.

A flustered Lois followed. The mystery author grabbed for the leash, but the Shiba Inu was too quick for her.

Watson bolted for the stairs, and Reynard eagerly chased him.

Faith wasn't about to let her cat disappear again. She took the stairs two at a time. Her mother and Lois followed.

Watson vaulted the final step to the second floor and ran down the hallway.

"Watson!" Faith called.

At the same time, Lois yelled for Reynard to sit.

The dog still hadn't learned that command, and Watson was too busy running to pay attention to Faith.

The chase continued.

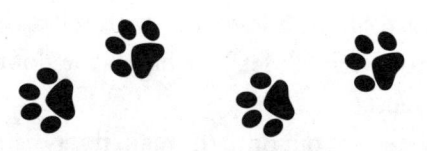

The cat was stiff from being cramped in the musty box. What he really wanted was another solid meal and a comfortable nap in his favorite

chair, but the annoying fox-like dog had to instigate a game of tag. He raced down a hallway, realizing too late that he had entered a dead end.

A door began to open. He dashed through the gap as if his life depended upon escaping, although the worst the dog would do was muss up his already filthy fur with a slobbery doggy kiss.

The dog tried to follow him inside.

But the tall man blocked the opening with his leg. "Oh no, mister. No dogs allowed in my room."

It was the man who had stolen his rattle toy. The cat hopped onto the arm of a chair. Then he noticed the man held the toy in his hand, so he batted at the man's arm, hoping he would drop the toy.

Instead, the tall man lifted the toy out of reach. "No cats either." He scooped the cat up with one arm. His grasp was firm but gentle.

He meowed indignantly.

"Watson?" His human poked her head through the open doorway.

Oh, sure, she was quick to rescue him now. Where had she been when he was locked in the box? He huffed, then took another swipe at the rattle toy.

"Miss Newberry, I was just coming to find you." The tall man held out the rattle toy to her.

This was good. His person would bring his toy home, saving him the trouble of carrying it through the manor and across the grounds to the cottage.

Faith was astonished at how quickly a crowd materialized, drawn by the excitement of Reynard chasing Watson, but the guests were only adding to the chaos. Rose was among the curious gathering in the hallway, along with Lois and Hannah. Lois grabbed her dog's leash.

"Did someone find the fifth treasure?" one guest asked.

"No, it's Lois's dog again," another answered.

Faith reached for her cat, cradled in Damian's arm.

Instead, the tall man handed her a packet of envelopes brittle with age, tied together with a faded, tattered ribbon.

As Faith accepted the packet, it rattled. "What is this?"

"I'm not certain." Damian glanced at the throng crowded around his open door. "Come inside. Miss Fairwell, please join us."

"May my mother come in too?" Faith asked him.

"Certainly. This concerns her as well."

Rose turned to the crowd. "This isn't about the hidden treasure. You'll have to hunt elsewhere."

Damian held the door open for them.

As Faith stepped by him, she was again struck by his height. He was taller than Wolfe by several inches.

The Charles Dickens Suite was elegantly appointed with its ornate brass bed, fireplace, standing mirror, and a replica of one of the famed author's desks. The heavy brocade curtains were drawn back to reveal a lovely view of the topiary garden.

When everyone was inside, Damian closed the door firmly and set Watson on the bed. "Please take a seat."

Faith and her mother sat on the love seat, but Rose remained standing, a troubled look on her face.

Faith was baffled by Damian's serious tone. Was he about to confess to murder? She studied the packet of envelopes he had handed to her. *Jane Newberry* was scrawled across the top envelope. She almost gasped. These were the envelopes Laura had seen.

"Your cat was playing with that packet of envelopes in the hallway the other day," Damian said. "I thought it was part of the cache of heirloom seeds and rose stock I received during an estate sale while Lionel was renovating a garden." His face twisted briefly into a grimace. "The so-called Hortense Danford rose was my find."

17

"But Lionel found the heirloom rose," Faith's mother responded. "Isn't that what he said at the opening breakfast?"

"Lionel took credit for many discoveries made by his staff," Damian said with a hint of bitterness. "I was at the sale on Lionel's behalf, but the estate owner specifically gave me the box. I naively told Lionel about the rare rose stock. He insisted that because I received the items while acting as an employee of Foille Enterprises, the company was the rightful owner of the box."

"That hardly seems fair," Rose said.

"It gets worse," Damian continued. "In a fit of generosity, Lionel let me keep the rest of its contents, but he took the rose stock. He promised I could name it after my grandmother. Right up until he announced he was naming it the Hortense Danford."

Ouch, Faith thought.

Damian was seething with anger that Lionel had named the rose instead of allowing him to name it after his beloved grandmother. Had he been angry enough to kill?

Faith shifted uneasily on the love seat. She and her mother might be sitting in the presence of a murderer.

"At least you salvaged something." Rose pointed to the packet in Faith's hands. "From the rattling noise, those sound like seed packets. Were they in the box from the estate sale?"

"At first, I thought they were," Damian said. "The estate's owner knew I could use a box of old seeds and tools for an inner-city gardening project, so he set them aside for me. Free materials are always welcome." He tapped a finger on the packet in Faith's hands.

Watson's ears pricked up at the rattling.

"I didn't remember that being in the box, but it was a jumbled mess," Damian continued. "When I saw your cat playing with the packets in the hallway, I assumed they were mine, so I took them back. However, I couldn't imagine how he'd gotten ahold of them in my room."

"Cats can be creative," her mom said.

Faith scanned the room, searching for evidence of a secret passage. Watson had a talent for finding his way in and out of the most unlikely places. Except for old sea chests.

Damian glanced from Faith to her mother. "When I opened one of the envelopes, I realized they might all contain rare treasures. Although how I could have overlooked these the whole time I've had the box is beyond me." He shook his head. "Then I learned your name is Newberry, and I read the outside of the envelopes."

Rose leaned close, examining the packets. "That's the name on the top envelope in the stack. The ink is faded, but you can still read it. *Jane Newberry.*"

"What a coincidence." Her mother explained to Damian and Rose how Watson had gone missing, then was found in a hidden room inside a Newberry sea chest presumably dating from the 1800s.

"Is it possible Watson could have found the envelopes in the chest and brought them downstairs?" Rose asked. "Obviously it was before he got locked inside."

"That makes more sense." Damian regarded Watson, who seemed to be paying close attention to the conversation.

"Watson wandered off numerous times during this retreat," Faith said. "I thought he was spending his time with Betsy, but he might have been exploring the chest." She shook the stack of envelopes. "They sound like they could be full of buttons. Would it hurt if I peeked inside one?"

"Not as long as they stay dry," Damian said. "The one I opened was labeled 'lemon balm.' I didn't open any others, but they appear to be vegetables and medicinal herbs."

Faith carefully untied the ribbon and eased an envelope out of the stack. *Carrot* was printed in neat script, faded with age. She turned it over. A disk of wax with the initial *N* sealed the envelope. Faith slid a fingernail under the wax, then lifted the flap and peered inside. She held the envelope open so the others could see the contents—seeds.

"Those must belong to your family," Rose said.

Damian nodded. "And if that chest has been undisturbed for over a century, those seeds are a rare treasure."

"If they're a hundred years old, surely they aren't still viable," her mother remarked.

"Seeds stored in the right conditions can last hundreds, even thousands of years," Rose said. "A two-thousand-year-old date seed from Masada was once grown into a successful plant. Viable seeds that old are incredibly rare, but I think it's worth at least testing these."

"Your seeds are worth their weight in gold," Damian said. "No, they're worth more. Far more."

"Oh dear." Mom covered her mouth with one hand, as though afraid to say anything else.

"What is it?" Faith asked her.

"A valuable cache of Newberry seeds was hidden away in Castleton Manor for a century. Your father's ancestors might have been counting on receiving those seeds."

Great, Faith thought. *Another reason to revive Dad's suspicions about the Jaxon family deliberately ruining the Newberry family all those generations ago.*

"There must be some other explanation," Faith said. "If the Jaxons stole the trunk from the Newberrys, then why did they preserve it so carefully? Wouldn't they want to get rid of the evidence?"

"The seeds certainly would have been important when they were shipped," Rose said. "But their value wouldn't have been anywhere near what it is today. No one would have thought to preserve them for future generations."

"As it is," Damian said, "we won't know if these will germinate until they're tested. They may have been exposed to damp conditions on the trip across the Atlantic. Or the trunk could have been stored in a hot barn loft or a wet basement and moved to the hidden room later. We have to be realistic. The seeds may not sprout."

"We're not absolutely certain they came from the chest Watson discovered," Faith reminded them. "I wish my cat could talk. He could let us know where he found them." She studied Watson.

He blinked slowly.

That was typically a sign that he agreed, but with what? That he had gotten the seeds from the sea chest, or he wished he could talk? Faith studied the stack of packets. "How can we be sure these belong to my family?"

"Charlotte is asking the curator of the whaling museum to examine the trunk," Faith's mother said. "Perhaps he could check the authenticity of the envelopes as well."

"That's a good idea." Faith held out the envelopes to Damian. "Please keep them until Mr. Bennett can study them."

Damian shook his head. "I discovered a treasure once and naively gave it to someone I trusted. I won't put you in the same position."

"I respect your honesty," her mother said. "You could have kept those seeds, made up some story about how you came by them, and claimed the treasure and the glory for yourself."

Faith noticed the admiring way Rose gazed at Damian.

"I would appreciate it if you'd keep these for now," her mother continued. "After Mr. Bennett verifies the date of the envelopes, perhaps you can help my husband determine how to have them tested, so we can see if there's any life in the seeds after all this time."

"Thanks for your trust in me." Damian accepted the packet from Faith, cradling the brittle envelopes in his hands. "I'll place them in the manor safe. They'll be secure there." He picked up a large manila envelope and carefully slid the seed envelopes inside.

"If the seeds are as important as you say, we should all go together," Mom suggested. "Like a scientific expedition."

"A botanical expedition," Rose said with a smile.

Watson lifted a paw and batted the new envelope in Damian's hands.

"Yes," Faith agreed. "An expedition to keep the seeds out of the paws of cats." *And book thieves.* If only Faith had been wise enough to place Jeremiah's book in the safe.

As they left Damian's room, Faith was relieved that the guests had listened to Rose and gone elsewhere to search for the day's hidden treasure. Unfortunately, when Faith led Damian, Rose, and her mother down the wide, carpeted stairs, she could see the crowd had merely moved to the lobby.

Throngs of guests bustled around below them, some on their hands and knees, searching every nook and cranny, even pushing through the lush foliage of potted plants. Animals joined their humans, yipping, mewing, and squawking in shared excitement.

Watson squirmed in Faith's arms, anxious to join the melee. She held him tight.

Marlene stood in the middle of the flight of carpeted stairs, looking a bit like a conductor who had lost control of the orchestra.

"What's going on?" Faith asked Marlene.

"One of the guests decided the fifth treasure must be hidden near the safe." Strands of Marlene's hair had escaped her typically tidy style, and the skirt of her beige suit was marred by paw prints. "It's been utter chaos ever since. I've been trying to convince people to move along to the next session, but they won't budge. You'd think they were hunting for a treasure chest full of doubloons, not a basket of books and seeds."

Faith noticed Damian clutch the manila envelope closer to his chest.

"The clue did mention being locked up," her mother said.

"Mary was referring to Colin," Faith said. "He was kept in his secluded bedroom. I'm surprised someone thought of the safe."

Three guests approached the clerk at the front desk. An animated discussion ensued, punctuated by sharp yips from a miniature dachshund. It appeared the guests wanted to come behind the desk to search for the treasure. The clerk held up his hands to stop them.

"There's no getting near the front desk," Rose said. "Not without making a scene."

Damian thrust the envelope toward Faith. "You're in a position of authority. The guests will make way for you."

Faith smiled. "Librarians only have command over their books. Besides, the seeds have been safe in your room so far. You can bring them down later after the guests have found the prize."

"I don't think I have a choice." As Damian turned to climb the stairs, he collided with Hannah. The manila envelope fell on the steps as he grabbed her arm to keep her from falling. "Excuse me."

"No, I'm sorry. It was my fault." Hannah picked up the envelope. It rattled as she handed it to Damian. Then she rushed down the stairs, veering off across the lobby and avoiding the crowd.

Damian continued his trek up the stairs.

Rose waded into the crowd, uttering calming words and firm suggestions to take their search elsewhere.

Watson squirmed, nearly escaping Faith's arms.

"Do you want me to take Watson to the cottage?" her mother asked.

"Thanks, but maybe some treasure hunters will follow us to the library if I open it," Faith responded. "I'd better keep Watson with me, or he might run back here."

Mom patted her shoulder and gave Watson a quick ear rub. "I'll go back to the hidden room. Maybe Mr. Bennett has arrived by now. Your father may need emotional support if he learns that it truly is a Newberry sea chest."

Faith refused to set Watson down until they were safely inside the library.

He inspected every inch of the spacious room as though making sure nothing had changed in his absence. In reality, he had been missing only two nights, but it had felt like an eternity to Faith. She couldn't imagine what it had felt like to her cat.

With all the stress of his absence and the relief of being reunited with him, Faith wanted nothing more than a long nap. Instead, she assisted guests with research or finding the next good fiction read.

Between tasks, she checked on Watson. After being confined in a sea chest, he seemed eager to stretch his legs. He climbed the narrow stairs to the second level of the library a dozen times, chasing a crumpled piece of scrap paper that hadn't made it into the trash can.

Around midafternoon, Jeremiah walked in with Sage perched on his shoulder. The owl took in the scene with round orange eyes and hooted.

Watson went over to Jeremiah and rubbed against his legs.

He reached down to scratch behind Watson's ears. "Hey, kitty. I heard you were missing. Good to see you back."

Faith was bursting to tell Jeremiah the news about the heirloom seeds, but nothing had been verified. It might be better to wait until Damian had determined whether or not the seeds were still viable.

"Has my book turned up?" Jeremiah asked.

"Not yet." Faith didn't like disappointing the forest gardener, but there had been no word about the missing book. "Was Ms. Russell able to assist you?"

"She called the police," Jeremiah said. "I filed a report. My insurance might cover the cost, but money's not the issue. That book is a rare treasure trove of information about Colonial-era plants and the Pennacook Native American people. Even so, I doubt many guests here would want it badly enough to commit a crime to get it."

"I disagree," Faith said. "Lois could use it for research on native plants for her mystery novels. Hannah might want to learn about early organic farming."

"Hannah?" Jeremiah grimaced.

Sage flapped his one good wing.

"Hannah's almost militant about organic gardening," Faith replied.

Jeremiah glanced around the library, then leaned closer to Faith's desk. "She talks the talk, but she was outed for spraying her crops with pesticides a few years ago."

"That's not what I heard," Faith said. "She told me Lionel sprayed a flower garden next door to her farm and the chemicals got on her plants. She lost her organic certification for two years and nearly lost her farm."

"No, it's the other way around. Lionel reported her. I don't like to gossip, but it's a fact." Jeremiah checked his watch. "I need to head to my next talk. Will you let me know if you hear anything about the book?"

"Yes, of course."

After he'd left, Faith pulled her notebook out of a drawer and began writing. Jeremiah couldn't have used the old book with a chapter on poisonous plants to attempt killing Hannah, because it was missing. Unless he was just covering up the fact that he had poisoned Hannah using information from the book and then had hidden the evidence.

Her mind whirled with the possibilities. But one thing was certain. Someone was lying. Was it Hannah or Jeremiah?

18

Marlene entered the library, walking purposefully to the wall where Faith was shelving books. She had regained her composure after the chaos in the lobby earlier that day. Her hair was impeccably neat once more, and her skirt was free of paw prints. "I'm glad you found your cat. I know how attached you are to him."

"Thank you." Faith knew Marlene was not a pet person, so her words were especially comforting. "I'm so relieved he's back."

Watson strolled over and rubbed against Marlene's ankles.

The assistant manager bent down and awkwardly patted him on the head.

Faith hid a smile. "Did a guest find today's treasure?" she asked.

"It was in the pet spa," Marlene said, irritation coloring her words. "Nowhere near the front desk."

Faith snapped her fingers. "Of course! Locked up. The spa has kennels for the pets while they're waiting to be groomed or massaged."

Marlene patted her hair, as though the mere recollection of the rowdy crowd of treasure hunters was enough to muss up her style. "If only they'd thought of that earlier. Nevertheless, order has been restored."

"What was the treasure?" Faith asked.

"Pet gifts," Marlene said. "A padded bed, ceramic food and water dishes, seeds for catnip and indoor edible grass, that sort of thing. But that's not what I came to tell you."

Faith braced herself. Marlene might have news about Jeremiah's book. Or maybe a guest had complained about Watson and Reynard racing through the manor. It would be a shame for Watson to be banished so soon after regaining his freedom from the chest.

"One of the guests spoke to me after hearing about the missing book," Marlene said. "She noticed someone rummaging through your desk while Laura was distracted with several pushy guests."

"Why didn't this guest stop the thief?" Faith asked.

"She had no way of knowing whether the person had permission to retrieve an item from your desk," Marlene said. "The missing book wasn't announced until last night's dinner. And she noted the person acted with total confidence in front of a crowd."

"That's a classic way to deflect suspicion. Who was it? Did you get the book?"

Marlene sighed. "That's the problem. The guest could tell it was a woman, but she wore a scarf, sunglasses, and a raincoat."

"Sunglasses and a raincoat inside? You're kidding. That should have caught the attention of everyone in the manor."

"Don't forget that several guests were badgering Laura at the time. The spotlight was on her." Marlene folded her arms across the front of her beige jacket. "I'm certainly looking forward to the conclusion of this disastrous gardening retreat."

Faith was not anxious for it to end. She still didn't know who'd stolen the book and whether the culprit had used information in the book to poison Hannah.

And she still had no idea how Lionel had died.

After locking the library that afternoon, Faith picked up Watson and carried him out of the manor. Halfway to the gardener's cottage, the cat squirmed to be let down. Faith reluctantly set him on the grass. What if he disappeared into one of the lush gardens?

Watson dashed ahead, then sat on the stoop and waited for her to open the door.

Faith smiled. "Oh, you just wanted to get home faster."

Faith's mother was sitting on the sofa in the living room when they walked in. She glanced up from the novel she was reading. "It's good to see you happy."

"Watson is back. I'm positively ecstatic." Faith glanced around the cozy room. "Where's Dad?"

"He's still talking with the museum director about the sea chest. It was fascinating watching them unpack it piece by piece. All that dust, though. I needed a break." Her mom stood. "I made iced tea. Would you like a glass?"

"That sounds great."

The two women moved into the kitchen.

Watson sat in the center of the floor and meowed.

"You deserve a treat for staying with me all afternoon." Faith retrieved a tunaroon from the cupboard and gave it to her cat.

Watson inhaled the treat, then meowed again.

"I just gave you one," Faith said.

"He's making up for the meals he missed while he was stuck in that trunk." Her mother set two glasses filled with ice on the kitchen table, then poured cold tea from a pitcher into them.

"I'm so relieved he's back." Faith sighed. "If having a cat is this stressful, I can't imagine having children. I'd be a wreck."

"Worrying shows you care," her mom said. "At some point, though, you have to trust in the higher power to watch over your babies. Difficult situations will occur. That's part of life. But you will get through them."

They sat at the table and sipped iced tea in companionable silence while Watson groomed his face. Faith treasured the quiet moment. Watson's episode proved how suddenly everything could change. She said a silent prayer of thanks.

The front door opened, and her father burst into the kitchen, full of excitement. "So far, Mr. Bennett believes Josiah Newberry's trunk and its contents date to the 1880s. Castleton Manor was completed in 1895. The trunk could have been stored anywhere until it was moved to the manor. Mr. Bennett agreed it was odd to find it hidden on the third floor of the manor when it appears to belong to Josiah Newberry."

"That mystery will have to wait," her mother said. "You need to change for dinner."

Dad groaned. "Can't we have a quiet dinner here?"

"We're eating with Jenna, Nick, and Oliver again," Mom reminded him. "They're excited about going to The Captain's Table."

"That's another thing," he said. "We had fun at that little seafood place we ate at last night."

"There isn't a table large enough for all of us," Barbara said. "Eileen and the Jaxons are joining us too. We may not be wealthy, but we can afford an occasional dinner at a nice restaurant."

Her father waved his hands. "The Jaxons move in a different world than the Newberrys. I can't possibly hope to keep up."

Mom tilted her head. "What's wrong?"

Dad reached for Mom's hand. "We're comfortable but only because we've been good about watching our pennies."

"No one expects us to match the Jaxons' lifestyle," her mother said. "I agree that we've been going a little overboard this week, but we can rein things in again when we go home."

"That's good. We can't afford eating out all the time. Besides, I love your cooking." He patted his stomach. "There's just one thing..."

"What is it, dear?"

"The wedding." Her father paused. "I wanted to pay for the whole show, like I did for Jenna. It's a father's duty and privilege. It's tradition. But the shindig you and Charlotte are planning is far beyond our means." He glanced at Faith. "Here we are discussing your life as if you're still a child. You have the final say in this."

Faith chewed on her lower lip for a moment, thinking about how to say how she felt in the most diplomatic way possible.

"A wedding is a once-in-a-lifetime event," her mother said.

"I know," Faith replied. "And I know the Jaxons can afford to pay for the entire wedding. So this is not about money. It's just that both Wolfe and I would be content with a simple ceremony and reception." The disappointment on her mother's face nearly made Faith stop, but she had more to say, and now was the time. She focused on her father. "On the other hand, I understand that the Jaxons feel an obligation to share the wedding with family and business connections."

"It's your day," her dad said. "You should get what you want."

"I've been ridiculous." Her mom dabbed a tissue to her eyes. "Your father is right. You should have the wedding you want, not the one your mother and future mother-in-law decide on."

Faith placed a hand on her mother's shoulder. "There is a middle ground. Maybe we can simplify some of the peripheral plans, like the rehearsal and reception dinners, and still keep the elegance of the ceremony."

Her mother placed her hand over Faith's. "That sounds like a good compromise. Now, let's get ready for dinner."

Faith went to her room to change.

Watson trotted behind her, then hopped lightly onto the bed. He threw himself onto his side and stretched his full length across an afghan Eileen had knitted. Faith could hear his purring across the room.

"I wish I could stay here with you," she told the cat. "It's easy to make you happy. How do I get what I want without disappointing my mother?"

Dinner at The Captain's Table was more fun than Faith had anticipated. Jenna told Wolfe and Charlotte stories from her and Faith's childhood, generating many laughs.

Faith described Watson's imprisonment in the sea chest and the discovery of the old seed packets. Her father explained the careful examination of the contents of the chest. Everyone speculated on how it could have been walled up inside a secret room for so long.

Faith slept soundly that night with Watson curled by her side.

When she woke Saturday morning, clear skies promised another beautiful August day.

Watson raced Faith to the kitchen.

Her father appeared in the doorway, then glanced behind him before tiptoeing into the kitchen. "Last day," he whispered. He reached down to pat Watson's head. "Morning, boy."

"You and Mom will be staying through the weekend," Faith said, keeping her voice low. "It's the last day of the retreat, but not the last day we get to visit."

"I should have been more specific." He raised his notebook. "I'm talking about Lionel's murder. This is the last day all our suspects will be present."

Faith smiled. "We'd better hurry if we want to compare notes. Mom will be up soon." She pulled her notebook out of her bag. "Here's my new information."

After they sat down at the table, Faith told her father about her conversation with Jeremiah and the book he had ordered. She mentioned that the book had a chapter on native poisonous plants. Then she related that Laura was in charge of the library when the book disappeared and that a guest had seen a woman in an obvious disguise rummaging through Faith's desk at the time the book went missing.

"A person could get information about poisonous plants off the Internet," her dad said. "The book may not be relevant."

"Doesn't it seem coincidental that it went missing right before Hannah was poisoned?" Faith asked.

"Perhaps. But I think we can safely cross Damian off our suspect list."

"Because a woman was seen stealing the book?"

He rubbed his chin. "From the way Rose and Damian interacted on a panel discussion yesterday, I'd say they were sweet on each other."

Faith patted her father's arm. "That's old news. You didn't need to sneak into the kitchen to tell me that."

Her father grinned. "You said Damian had time before his trip to the hospital to commit the murder."

"Can you account for his time?" Faith asked.

He nodded.

"How?"

"Your mother dragged me to a talk in the salon yesterday. I got sleepy halfway through learning about Victorian gardens in classic literature and nearly dozed off. So I left to stretch my legs and get a breath of fresh air. I stepped outside onto the loggia and almost into the middle of a conversation between Officer Rooney and Marlene. I ducked behind a potted plant."

"Very James Bond," Faith remarked.

Dad smiled, clearly enjoying the comparison. "Marlene was telling Officer Rooney that she'd most likely find Damian wherever Rose was."

"What else did they say?" she asked.

"Marlene told Rooney that Damian and Rose were sitting by the Peter Pan fountain the first day at two o'clock and they didn't move for an hour. She complained that the two had been inseparable since that tête-à-tête. Her words, not mine. Damian was on panel discussions from three to five, and then the lovebirds went for a stroll through the Victorian garden until dinner. Marlene doesn't miss anything."

"True," Faith said. "She's very observant."

"According to your information, Damian's whereabouts are accounted for during the time frame of Lionel's murder."

Faith sat back. "I'm really glad to hear that. He seems like such a nice man, but I've been worried he might be guilty."

"A jury has to presume a suspect is innocent until proven guilty, but as a police officer, I had to presume anyone could be the perpetrator of a crime I was investigating."

"Jeremiah told me he was in a patch of forest during that time, but he has no witnesses. Other than his owl. Last I knew, Eileen hadn't verified whether Lois really volunteered with the literacy program. I haven't been able to confirm Hannah's alibi because Glenn isn't back from his fishing trip."

"Have you learned anything else?" her father asked.

Faith told him about Jeremiah's claim that it had been Hannah who had sprayed her own crops with pesticides and that Lionel had turned her in. "If he was telling the truth." She sighed. "Investigating a crime is hard work."

"It's a matter of assembling all the evidence." He held a finger to his lips. "I hear your mother."

They both scrambled to put away their notes.

By the time Faith's mother came in, they were both innocently sipping cups of coffee.

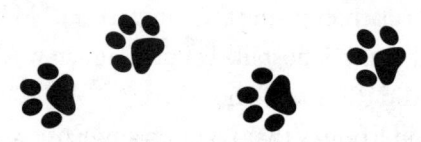

The breakfast buffet on the loggia that morning featured the British standards of scones and clotted cream, which fit with the sixth and final clue.

"Mary and Colin attempt to hide their growing health and appetites by having a hidden basket of food stashed near the garden," Rose said.

Guests jotted down notes. There would be intense competition to find the last hidden treasure.

"'You can trifle with your breakfast and seem to disdain your dinner if you are full to the brim with roasted eggs and potatoes and richly frothed new milk and oat-cakes and buns and heather honey and clotted cream,'" Rose continued, reading from *The Secret Garden*. "I will give you one hint. The treasure is not hidden in the kitchen."

Guests speculated about where the treasure would be found. Many latched on to the idea that the prize would be in a picnic basket.

Life returned to normal in most ways. Except for the unsolved murder, of course. Watson accompanied Faith to work and curled up on a chair in front of the fireplace. Faith answered questions and helped guests find books, stealing glances toward her cat to make sure he was really there and her nightmare was over.

A woman with short white hair approached the desk, leading a Devon rex on a pink leash. The cat's neck was circled with a sequin-spangled collar. Or perhaps the sequins were real gemstones. Both the woman and her cat were impeccably groomed and carried themselves like royalty.

Watson hopped off his chair to meet the unique cat.

Faith greeted the woman. "Good morning. How may I help you?"

"At breakfast, Rose announced the clue for the sixth and final treasure. I would love to be the one to find it. Where is the kitchen?"

"Rose clearly stated the treasure is not in the kitchen." Faith could only imagine Brooke's reaction to guests wandering anywhere near her domain.

"Not *in* the kitchen," the woman said, "but it could be *near* the kitchen."

"There are many places where food is served," Faith said. "The breakfast room, the banquet hall, and the loggia. Then there was the picnic—"

"Today is the last day of the retreat," an older gentleman in a lightweight summer jacket interrupted. "Someone has to find it before the end of the day."

"The use of *The Secret Garden* as the basis for clues to find hidden prizes was quite clever." The woman sighed. "But with only six prizes, most of us are bound to be disappointed."

The man touched her arm. "But getting the opportunity to stay at Castleton Manor is truly a prize worth winning."

The two guests left together to attend a talk in one of the many gardens.

Later Wolfe arrived in the library unexpectedly and gave Faith one of his dazzling smiles, his blue eyes full of mischief. "I brought you a little something, and I think you'll find it quite interesting."

19

Wolfe placed a cloth-wrapped parcel on the desk with care. He unwrapped the cloth, revealing an old book.

Faith hoped it was Jeremiah's missing book, but she knew instantly it wasn't. She had seen similar books in Wolfe's third-floor library, the leather covers worn and the pages yellowed.

"A captain's logbook? Is it my great-great—however many greats, I lose track. My distant grandfather's?"

"I'm afraid it's not Josiah Newberry's." He pulled a chair beside the desk. "I couldn't sleep last night, thinking about that sea chest Watson found."

At the sound of his name, the cat raised his head. He trotted over to Wolfe, rubbing against his trouser legs.

Wolfe reached down and scratched Watson's neck. "Yes, you found the trunk, but don't let being a hero go to your head."

Watson purred.

"As I was saying, I kept thinking about the chest. When Mr. Bennett unpacked it, he didn't find a captain's log. It's clearly Josiah Newberry's trunk, but how did it get on the third floor?"

Faith thought ruefully that her father would dearly love the answer to that question.

"I scoured my library for any bills of lading for Angus Jaxon's ship during that time period," Wolfe continued. "May I borrow a pair of your gloves? I left mine upstairs."

Faith retrieved a pair of white gloves and gave them to Wolfe.

He put on the gloves, then opened the book to a page marked with a slip of acid-free paper. "Here's the entry written a few weeks after your relative passed away. News traveled slowly then."

Faith nodded.

"I skimmed ahead to see if there was any mention of the trunk. This paper was tucked between pages of the log." Wolfe carefully opened the fragile old paper. "It's a ship's manifest. There are no other cargo lists in the log, so Angus must have thought this one was of particular importance."

Faith stared at Wolfe, confused. "A sea chest. Josiah Newberry's?" This would not make her father happy. The list seemed to confirm the family legend that after Josiah Newberry had died, Angus Jaxon had stolen the Newberry family fortune.

"Hang on." Wolfe flipped to another marked page in the book. "The sea chest was stored near the docks, waiting to be claimed by Newberry's relatives."

"I see that." Faith read the words several times. "Why wouldn't they claim the trunk? Surely they would have wanted Josiah's last effects."

"That we may never know with certainty," Wolfe said. "I would like to believe every reasonable effort was made to contact them. Back then, communication was erratic at best. Maybe they never got the message."

"Or maybe," Faith said slowly, "they did get the message. Remember, they suspected Angus of foul play. They could have been so angry that they ignored his attempt to return the chest." She imagined a Newberry ancestor ripping up a letter from Angus Jaxon or pitching it into a hearth fire. Tears filled Faith's eyes. "It's so sad to think of all the bad blood between our families."

Wolfe placed his gloved hand over Faith's and squeezed. "Until now." He lifted his hand and regarded the contaminated glove. "I'm guessing you would call that a rookie mistake."

Faith laughed. He had a way of lifting her spirits.

Wolfe smiled at her, then used his other hand to close the book.

"Dad might not understand what this means," Faith said. "I don't understand it either."

"The best-case scenario is that the sea chest ended up on the third floor in the belief that the Jaxons and Newberrys would reconcile one day. If Angus had really been plotting against Josiah, he wouldn't have gone to the trouble to preserve the chest."

"As far as he knew, the contents were of little value," Faith said. "The seeds wouldn't have meant to people then what they mean today."

Her heart broke a little as she thought about a wife waiting for special seeds from the old country. Instead, she'd lost both her husband and the seeds. Or had she been so bitter about her husband's demise that she refused to pick up the trunk with the seeds?

"We can only speculate." Faith sighed. "It's so sad how their unhappy ending affected the next several generations."

"Our happy ending won't change the past." Wolfe wrapped an arm around Faith's shoulders and kissed her temple. "But think of the bright future our wedding will create for both our families."

By midmorning, the library was quiet again. Faith locked the door and met her parents in the lobby. It was such a treat, spending time with them. They chatted as they strolled toward a remote pocket garden near the cliffs.

"What a wonderful idea," her mother said, "setting a talk on pet-friendly gardening in a setting where animals can relax."

A long arbor heavy with Concord grapevines shaded rows of chairs. A white picket fence surrounded the pocket garden. Watson walked beside Faith and entered the garden as she held open the gate. Even though Betsy attended, Watson chose to sit on Faith's lap, which pleased her to no end.

During the talk, more than one pet owner exclaimed about a

houseplant or a landscaping plant he or she had not known was toxic to a furry friend. Faith had the impression that many plants were going to be removed from gardens after attendees learned of their potential hazards to their animal companions.

At the end of the talk, guests filed toward the gate.

When Mom approached the speaker to ask a question, Dad pulled Faith aside. "Is that the boathouse keeper's truck?" he whispered.

Faith tried to be subtle as she looked toward Glenn's cottage, surrounded by leafy trees. It sat at the top of a steep hill, with a view of the boathouse below. "Yes, it is." She pulled out her cell phone. "He must be back from his fishing trip."

"Wait. I'll take your mother back to the manor. She doesn't realize I'm working a case, and I'd like to keep it that way."

Faith smiled. "I agree. The boathouse isn't far. I'll walk over."

The day was toasty warm, but a cool breeze from the ocean made the walk pleasant. Faith felt a peace she hadn't known for days. She smiled at Watson, trotting beside her.

He glanced up and mewed as if he knew what she was thinking and agreed.

Glenn lowered the tailgate of his pickup. His weathered face, or what she could see of it above his long black whiskers, was pink with sun. A fisherman's hat decorated with lures covered his short black hair. "Good morning. Had any good adventures lately, Watson?"

"Doesn't he always?" Faith asked. "Did you have a nice trip to New Hampshire?"

"The mosquitoes were biting, and the fish weren't." He lifted a cooler. "But I did manage to catch two lake trout and one salmon."

Watson meowed at the mention of the fish.

"Salmon?" Faith asked. "In New Hampshire?"

"You bet. They're not like the Alaskan fish everyone thinks of, but they taste just as nice. I've got to put these away. Come on in."

Faith followed Glenn into his spacious cottage. The back steps led to a tidy kitchen with feminine touches. Blue gingham curtains, crocheted hot pads, and chair seat pads in a print that matched a homemade tablecloth softened the bright-white walls and cabinets.

"Excuse the mess," Glenn said. "The missus has been out of town taking care of her mother. She's arriving home this afternoon, with two of the grandkids in tow."

"I think your kitchen is lovely," Faith assured him.

Glenn opened the cooler and removed three large fish from a bed of crushed ice. They had been gutted, but they still had their heads and tails.

Watson wound around Glenn's ankles, intensely interested.

Glenn rinsed the fish, then dug out plastic wrap and began packaging two for the freezer. "I'll cook the salmon, and maybe fry some potatoes and onions. My wife will appreciate having dinner ready when she gets home. She'll have her hands full watching the children. She wasn't expecting me until tomorrow afternoon."

"That will be a nice surprise for her," Faith said.

After placing the wrapped fish in the freezer, Glenn grabbed a bag of potatoes and sat at the kitchen table with a knife.

"Let me help," Faith said.

Glenn handed her a knife, then pulled a frilly apron from a hook. "You'd better wear this. My wife would have a fit if she knew I let a lady help in the kitchen without offering her a proper apron to protect her clothes."

As they peeled and chopped, she told Glenn about the unexpected demise of Lionel on the first day of the retreat.

"Pity. I've seen his television show a few times. He seemed to know what he was talking about. How did the poor fellow pass?"

"He was murdered." Faith described how Lionel had been discovered draped over the biogas generator but had sustained an obvious head wound. "My father is a retired police sergeant, and he and I have been trying to figure out who might have killed him."

"I was out of state the past few days," Glenn said.

"Yes, and one suspect used you as an alibi." Faith explained Hannah's claim that Glenn had given her a ride to her farm on Monday afternoon when her car wouldn't start.

"Are you sure she was talking about me?" Glenn asked. "Maybe she had me confused with one of the gardeners, because I would remember giving someone a lift."

"She was very specific," Faith answered. "She must have known you'd be gone until the conference ended."

"That seems like a shaky way to set up an alibi," Glenn said. "Here. I'll take those potatoes." He scooped the potatoes off Faith's cutting board and into a bowl with his. He covered them with water and added a bit of salt. "Maybe she was hoping the trail would go cold before the police tracked her down. If she is the killer."

It was a possible solution to the mystery of Lionel's murder, but Faith had learned from past cases that the answer wasn't always obvious or simple. She mulled over several loose ends, taking the opportunity to talk it through with someone who was new to the case.

"Hannah isn't the only suspect." Faith briefly described the author, the forest gardener, and Lionel's employee. "Lois has an unconfirmed alibi for the time of the murder, but she also had a very strong motivation to kill Lionel. Jeremiah has no witnesses that he was in the woods when Lionel was killed. I've learned that Damian had reason to be angry with Lionel, but my father discovered he has an alibi too."

"My, my," Glenn said as he chopped an onion. "I hope you and your father can solve this puzzle."

"Me too, but we've only got the rest of today." Faith stood and untied the apron. "Thanks for listening. Your information has been helpful. It might be critical to the case."

"If there's anything else I can do, call me," Glenn said. "I'd hate to see someone get away with murder."

As Faith walked toward the manor with Watson at her side, she realized one thing didn't make sense. Hannah had either lied or been mistaken about Glenn driving her home Monday during Lionel's murder. If she had lied and she was the killer, who would have poisoned her Wednesday night? And why?

Faith needed to talk to her father. She studied the schedule. Her parents had mentioned their next destination was the Victorian tea.

In the Victorian garden, guests were seated at small tables featuring lacy cloths, delicate china dishes, and an assortment of goodies.

Her parents shared a table with two ladies wearing broad-brimmed hats decorated with ribbons and silk flowers. Her mother wore the hat she'd worn to the caterer tasting, the rose tulle and silk flowers matching her summer dress. Mom and the women were chatting, but Dad gazed off at some vague point in the distance, appearing acutely ill at ease to be trapped at a ladies' tea party.

Watson ran ahead of Faith and hopped lightly onto her mother's lap.

As Faith followed, Damian walked over and touched her arm. "I'm afraid I have some bad news."

Faith's heart thudded, not sure she could take more bad news this week. "What is it?"

"The Newberry seeds are missing."

20

Almost as though he had heard Damian's hushed words, her father looked their way.

Faith motioned for him to come over.

Damian waited until her dad joined them, then explained, "I retrieved the manila envelope from the safe. I was curious about which types of seeds had been sent to Jane Newberry, so I decided to create a list. Perhaps something really rare and sensational was in one of the packets."

Her father leaned closer to Damian. "What did you find?"

"Nothing."

Dad took a step back. "They aren't as important as you thought?"

"No," Damian said. "The envelope was full of ordinary vegetable seed packets. Modern ones. The old envelopes labeled with Jane Newberry's name had been replaced. The heirloom seeds are gone."

"How can that be?" Faith asked.

"Someone must have switched them between the time I returned the manila envelope to my room and when I took it to the manor safe later that day."

"Guests thought the Friday hidden treasure was near the manor safe," Faith told her father. "Dozens of people and pets crowded around the front desk. It was total chaos."

"And you just now discovered the seeds are gone?" her dad said.

Damian nodded.

"How long were they in your room?" Faith asked.

"You were with me when I left the lobby," Damian said to Faith. "I left the envelope in my room for the duration of two talks. Before dinner, I took it to the front desk, and the clerk placed it in the safe."

He grimaced. "I was so confident about it. Putting the envelope in the safe meant the seeds were secure. But I neglected to check the contents of the envelope. I was in a rush to meet Rose for dinner."

"Was your room locked?" her father asked. "From the time you returned the envelope to your room until you took it to the front desk?"

"Yes, although it hardly seems necessary here," Damian said.

Faith didn't have as much confidence that the manor was a safe haven. First Jeremiah's book and now her family's heirloom seeds had been stolen. Murder, lies, and thievery would taint the sterling reputation of the manor if they didn't solve the mystery soon.

Faith's father approached her mother, leaning close and whispering. She glanced at Faith and Damian with a concerned expression. Finally, she returned her attention to the other two women, seeming content to remain for the tea party.

"Let's go check it out," her dad suggested when he reached them once more.

The trio returned to the manor. On the second floor, Damian led Faith and her father down the hallway to his suite.

Her dad crouched to examine the lock. "No evidence of forced entry. Nothing amateurish, anyway."

Damian unlocked the door, and they entered the room.

Her father wore a stern expression as he searched for evidence. He stood at the window for a moment, then turned. "No balcony. The lock wasn't jimmied. Is there any other way a person might have entered the room?"

"Like a secret passageway?" Faith asked.

"After my daughter's cat was found inside a hidden room, it occurs to me that someone might have switched envelopes before you took the seeds to the manor safe." Dad stepped to the built-in bookcase, running his hands along the shelves. "And if they didn't come through a door or a window, a secret passageway is the only thing that makes sense." He pressed against a panel, and the bookcase swung a few inches away from the wall.

A soft tap came on the open door.

Her father quickly pushed the bookcase closed.

"Housekeeping." Laura poked her head inside.

"Just the person we needed," her dad said. "Who has access to guest rooms?"

"The housekeeping staff and Ms. Russell have master keys," Laura answered. "Is something wrong?"

"Damian believes a package may have been taken from his room," Faith said.

Laura's eyes grew wide. "Someone stole something from a guest's room?"

"I'm not sure what happened," Damian said.

"At the moment we're only checking to see who might have had access," her father said.

"No one in housekeeping would take something from a guest's room," Laura said. "Unless it was in a trash can. I'll ask Jennifer. She's the other housekeeper on duty. We can check the trash bags on our cleaning carts before we dump them."

"That's unlikely," her father said. "The package went missing yesterday. But it's probably a good idea to cover all the bases. Please keep this quiet for now. We don't want to alarm other guests until we're certain about the facts."

"You bet," Laura said before she left.

Faith turned to her father. His pensive expression reminded her this wasn't a random case of burglary. The loss of the seeds was deeply personal, threatening to sever a connection to his ancestors he had only established yesterday.

Faith's cell phone pinged. She checked her screen. "Dad, Wolfe wants us to join him for lunch."

"Right now?" Her father frowned. "We've got a situation."

"He wants to talk to us about the sea chest," Faith said. "We need to tell him about the missing seeds. Damian, would you join us?"

They took the elevator to the third floor in grim silence.

Wolfe's smile faded as they entered the Jaxon private quarters. "What's wrong?"

"I seem to be making a habit of losing treasures," Damian said. "The Newberry heirloom seeds are gone."

Wolfe steered them to the dining room, where a magnificent spread was laid out, but no one had much of an appetite. Her father and Damian filled Wolfe in on the details of the missing seeds and the bookcase door leading to a secret passage.

"I'm so sorry about this," Damian told her dad. "I'm devastated."

Faith felt her cheeks flush with regret and sympathy for Damian. "It's as much my fault as yours. Maybe more so. I could have taken them to my cottage or braved the crowd in the lobby to place them in the safe."

"Neither of you could have anticipated what would happen," Wolfe said. "Damian, you certainly didn't know about the secret door to your room."

"There was a talk about the history of the manor, including the secret passages," Faith said. "It's obvious someone figured out a way into your room and traded the envelope of heirloom seeds for the modern seeds before you took it to the safe."

"Who knew about the seeds?" Wolfe asked.

Faith recalled when Watson had taken refuge inside Damian's room. Guests had crowded into the hallway, curious about what had created the ruckus and probably hoping it had something to do with the hidden treasure.

"I remember seeing Lois and Hannah outside my door," Damian said.

"Along with several other guests," Faith said. "But no one knew what was in the envelopes."

"They might not look like modern seed packets," Damian said. "But many people attending this retreat could have guessed."

"None of them would have access to your room," Dad said.

"Unless they knew about the secret passage or got their hands on a master key."

"I suppose that's not impossible," Wolfe said. "Although I can't imagine even a clever thief getting Marlene's keys away from her."

"You placed the seed packets inside a manila envelope after the guests left," Faith said.

Damian shrugged. "The same crowd that was outside my door was in the lobby when I tried to take the seeds to the front desk. But they wouldn't know I had placed the packets in that envelope."

"We're not going to solve how the seeds left Damian's room right now," her father said. "Our priority should be finding where they went."

"I can verify whether anyone has checked out of the manor since the seeds disappeared," Wolfe offered. "The thief may still be here. We have to act fast. Most guests will be leaving after the final banquet tonight."

"It's a miracle the seeds survived this long." Dad grasped Faith's hand and squeezed. "I'll trust in another miracle that we'll find them again."

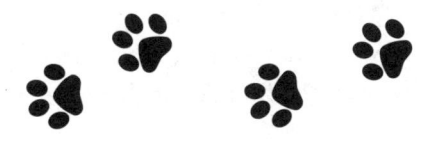

While her father and Damian drew up a plan to search for the seeds, Wolfe called Charlotte, and Faith brought Mom, Rose, and Watson upstairs, filling them in on the recent developments.

Finally, with a plan of action firmly in place, they broke into groups.

Faith's parents would pretend to be avidly searching for the sixth and final treasure. Charlotte would watch the front desk for guests checking out early. Damian recruited Rose to accompany him through the bookcase door in his room to learn where a thief might have entered the secret passage.

Wolfe and Faith headed for the guest parking lot, Watson

trotting beside them with his stubby tail pointing straight up. They agreed it seemed unlikely that a guest would place a stolen manila envelope filled with heirloom seeds in their vehicle in plain sight, but her dad firmly believed they needed to eliminate the obvious before digging deeper.

An hour later, when they checked in by text message, no one had discovered the seeds.

Let's regroup in the lobby, Wolfe suggested. *If we don't come up with something soon, we'll need to call the police.*

Faith's father hurried over to them, breathing hard. "I was nearly smacked over the head by an elderly guest who thought I was trying to steal a book out of her tote bag. Your mother suggested I stop searching so aggressively. Do you need help?"

"I just sent a message for our group to rendezvous," Wolfe said. "Faith and I didn't find anything either."

"Nothing out in the open," Faith said. "Apparently our thief isn't that foolish."

Her dad sighed. "At least we gave it a try."

"Watson!" Faith called. "We're leaving."

Instead of following, Watson headed toward the gardening shed. He meowed loudly over his shoulder at them before continuing on his trek.

"Maybe we should follow him," Wolfe said. "Watson has an uncanny knack for discovering clues to mysteries."

It wasn't his sixth sense that sent the cat to the building. It wasn't the earthy smell of gardening dirt and flower bulbs or the metallic and gasoline odors of lawn mowers either. No, it was a familiar sound. He couldn't see it, but he knew it was nearby.

A human carried his rattle toy. He almost hadn't heard it because it was wrapped inside a brown bag that made crunchy paper sounds. The human walked toward a tiny car.

The cat glanced over his shoulder to make certain his person and the others were following. Then he raced after the human with the rattle toy.

His person called the woman's name.

She paused, then turned slowly.

He did not like the look on her face. Not one little bit.

Faith watched Watson slow as he approached Hannah. The redhead carried a brown paper grocery bag. The cat circled her ankles, his focus on the bag.

Several clues aligned with shocking clarity, leaving Faith breathless. Her doubts melted away in an instant.

Lionel had nearly ruined Hannah, but it wasn't because he'd sprayed her crops with pesticide. Jeremiah was right. Lionel had discovered Hannah was guilty of that offense.

Hannah had not hitched a ride to her farm Monday with Glenn during the time of Lionel's murder.

Hannah had attended the talk where the secret passages of the manor were revealed. She was outside Damian's door when he handed Faith the heirloom seed packets, and she appeared on the stairs to jostle him, causing him to drop the manila envelope. After she figured out the envelope contained the valuable seeds, she discovered a secret way into his room and switched the packets.

She had lied about everything.

Liar. Thief. Murderer.

The only piece that didn't fit was why someone had poisoned her Wednesday night.

"Hannah," Faith said.

The farmer tore her glare from Watson to Faith. "Yes?" She was cool as a cucumber. "May I help you?"

"I believe that belongs to my family." Faith stepped over a coiled black watering hose, holding out her hand.

Hannah smiled as she raised the brown paper grocery bag. "I harvested sunflower seeds from the kitchen garden." She shook the bag, which rattled with the telltale sound of dry seeds. "Eban Matthews said it was okay."

"Really?" Faith asked. "And if I check with him, will he deny he spoke to you about sunflower seeds, just like Glenn denied he gave you a ride to your farm Monday?"

"I don't know what you're talking about." Hannah abruptly spun on her heel and continued on her way.

"Hold on. You aren't leaving until I see what's inside that bag." Faith expected her father to object. She probably didn't have the right to demand that Hannah open the bag, but she was desperate.

Besides, Watson had led them to the clue, and he was rarely wrong. In fact, Watson prowled behind the woman, never taking his eyes off the paper grocery bag.

Hannah's shoulders tensed under the colorful tunic she wore. When she whirled around to face Faith, she dropped the easygoing organic gardener facade. Hannah reached inside her tunic pocket and retrieved a plastic disposable lighter, which didn't seem ecologically sensitive to Faith. "Get away from me, or I'll torch the sunflower seeds."

"Why would we care if you torched some seeds, unless they're actually century-old seeds that belong to our family?" Faith's father stood beside her. "We know those are the heirloom seeds. The envelopes are addressed to my ancestor Jane Newberry. You stole them from Damian's room." His stern tone must have convinced many criminals to confess.

But not Hannah. Even though she seemed startled for a moment, she ignored the accusation and kept moving toward her car.

"You were at the talk Thursday morning about Castleton Manor," Faith said. "You heard about the secret passages and discovered one behind the bookcase. Right?" She glanced around to see Wolfe's reaction. *Where did he go?*

Her dad took a cautious step closer to Hannah. "Give us the seeds. We're going to have Damian test them for viability."

Faith felt faint with relief that her father still trusted Damian. She wasn't sure why she believed so firmly in his innocence, but she was glad her instincts aligned with her father's.

"Damian Winston?" Hannah snorted. "He doesn't know a petunia from a portulaca. He won't know what to do with these." She gave the bag another shake.

Watson stood on his hind legs and batted a paw against the brown paper.

"He was an apprentice to that phony know-nothing flower gardener Lionel." Hannah flicked the plastic lighter into flame and held it near the bag. "Do humanity a favor. Let me keep the seeds."

Faith took a step back, nearly tripping over the coiled watering hose. She heard the sound of a lawn mower roaring to life as she watched Hannah lower the lighter.

Hannah jerked open the driver's door and tossed the bag carelessly onto the passenger seat of the little car. She climbed in and slammed the door. She began backing up, then jerked to a halt. The car's windows lowered with a soft whirring. "Tell him to get out of my way!"

Wolfe sat on a riding lawn mower, parked squarely behind Hannah's car. He jumped off and strode to the car.

Hannah snatched up the paper bag and the lighter again. "I'll burn them."

"You don't really care about the environment, do you?" Faith asked.

"The heirloom seeds could be the find of the decade," her father said. "But you'd rather destroy them than see anyone else benefit from them. You won't let anything stand in the way of your own selfish plans. Even if you have to take a human life."

Hannah's face went pale. "Lionel had a heart attack and tripped over a flowerpot. That's how he ended up face-first over the biogas generator. It was a tragic accident." She seemed to regain her smug confidence, making it clear that she didn't think Lionel's death was the least bit tragic.

"That's not how it happened," Faith said. "Someone struck him with the handle of a garden hoe. A guest found the hoe and gave it to the police."

"That stupid treasure hunt made snoops out of everyone at the retreat," Hannah groused. "You can't walk two feet without running into someone poking the shrubs and prodding the flowerpots." She revved her car, threatening to back into the riding mower, but she seemed to realize the hopelessness of her situation. Instead, she slumped down in her seat.

"Maybe you didn't mean to kill Lionel when you struck him with the hoe," Faith said. "But you didn't help him when he fell on the biogas generator. Or did you take it a step further by opening the hopper, knowing the methane gas would asphyxiate him?"

"He tried to ruin me." Hannah banged a fist against the steering wheel. "I nearly lost my farm!"

In the middle of her tantrum, Hannah didn't notice Watson hop through the passenger window. He clamped his teeth onto the paper bag.

Faith had to keep Hannah distracted. "If you had lost your farm, it would have been due to your own actions. Lionel was doing what he thought was right by reporting you."

Watson struggled to lift the bulky paper bag. He wrestled with it, then toppled onto the floor and out of sight. The bag teetered on the edge of the seat.

"That's not true!" Hannah shrieked. "I would never poison my own crops. Lionel was only getting rid of his competition."

Hannah groped for the bag. Watson reached for it at the same time, but Hannah latched on to it first. She dangled the bag in front of her open window, taunting Faith. Then Hannah flicked her lighter and held it to a corner of the brown bag. Flames licked up the dry paper.

Faith screamed as the grocery bag containing the envelopes of precious heirloom seeds ignited.

21

Faith picked up the black garden hose and twisted the nozzle, praying that the faucet was on. With a jerk, water sprayed out of the nozzle and through the window of Hannah's car. Faith kept the hose aimed at the woman, hoping the cold water would douse her temper as well as the flames.

Hannah ducked inside the car with a shriek.

Watson tugged the scorched, wet paper bag out of Hannah's hand and tumbled out of the passenger window with it.

Hannah jerked the driver's door open. Screaming with rage, she charged at Faith, her hands raised like claws.

Wolfe and her father each caught one of Hannah's arms.

Eban ran up to them, waving his phone in the air. "I called the police when I realized what was happening. Then I started filming."

Watson trotted over to Faith, dragging his prize across the gravel driveway. The paper bag was a mess.

"You won't benefit from the seeds." Hannah's wild red hair hung in dripping hanks. She shook her head, sending a spray of water across Faith. "Nothing will ever grow from them. They're ruined."

Chief Garris treated Faith's father like a peer, listening carefully to his analysis of the situation while Officer Laddy took brief statements from Faith and Wolfe.

Hannah reverted to her mild-mannered organic gardener persona until Officer Rooney's probing questions triggered her red-hot anger.

The police handcuffed Hannah and took her away in one of the police cruisers. Dad rode in the other, clutching the ruined paper bag.

Wolfe escorted Faith to the lobby, where Mom, Charlotte, Rose, and Damian waited.

"What happened to Watson?" her mother asked. "He's all wet."

"So is Faith," Charlotte said. "Although not as wet as Watson."

"You should have seen Hannah," Wolfe said. "She got the worst of it."

Both mothers gaped at Faith and Wolfe.

"We'll explain everything," Faith said. "But first, I could really use a glass of iced tea. Why don't we all go to the cottage so Watson and I can clean up?"

As Faith bathed Watson in the kitchen sink, then dried him with towels, she and Wolfe detailed what had happened since his text message to meet in the lobby.

Damian began blaming himself again for the loss of the seeds.

"No one could foresee the events of the past week," Charlotte said. "Perhaps if you had not told the Newberrys about the seeds and kept them to yourself, they would be safe. But you made the proper decision by trying to return them to their rightful owners."

"You aren't responsible for Hannah's actions." Rose shook her head. "And here we all thought she was a mellow farmer."

"In the end, she didn't care about the seeds," Faith said. "She lied about not using pesticides and did whatever she could to cover up her secret. Including murdering Lionel."

"Where are the seeds?" Damian asked. "Was there anything left?"

"Faith's father has them," Wolfe said.

"Where is he?" Mom asked.

"Dad went with Chief Garris," Faith said. "He promised he'd be back in time for the final banquet."

"This was supposed to be a real vacation." Mom smiled. "But knowing your father, the highlight of the trip for him will be helping solve a case."

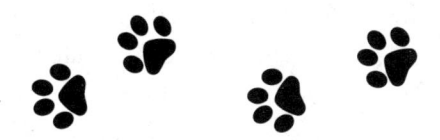

Faith showered and changed into a pale-green dress dotted with daisies she had been saving for the final dinner of the retreat. Mom wore a sleeveless silk dress in a shade of rose that matched her hat. She told Faith in a confidential tone that occasions to dress up would be rare when she returned home.

Faith should have felt like celebrating. The mystery of Lionel's death had been solved. Instead, she felt defeated. Hannah had insisted his death was an accident, but Faith suspected the police would learn the truth was much more sinister. The woman had a well-disguised streak of mean mixed with a hearty dose of crazy. If she couldn't have the heirloom seeds, she would rather see them destroyed than in the hands of anyone else.

Faith's cell phone rang. She smiled when she saw it was Eileen.

"I called the library in Glynde," her aunt said.

"And Lois was there as a volunteer from two to four," Faith finished for her.

"Did you call them already?" Eileen asked.

"No. Watson caught the murderer," Faith replied, then summarized the day's events.

"My word," Eileen said. "Watson deserves a whole pile of tunaroons for that."

Faith laughed. "I have no doubt he'll agree with you."

After Faith hung up, Mom insisted that Dad and Watson dress for the occasion. Watson tolerated a bow tie improvised from a bit of green ribbon to match his eyes. Dad wore a long-sleeved shirt with khakis, but the shirt was a dressy blue silk. He even agreed to a tie.

Her father escorted them to the loggia, and they sat down with Wolfe and Charlotte. The loggia was bright with solar-powered tiki torches and fairy lights. Flowers and herbs from the gardens scented the warm night air. Faith felt a bit melancholy, realizing it might be one of the last summer evenings they'd be able to dine outdoors without a sweater and one of the last times she'd dine with her parents as a single woman. Her spirits did improve a little at the thought of her upcoming wedding.

Almost as though he read her thoughts, Wolfe reached for her hand.

Faith turned at the sound of Betsy's whirring electric wheelchair. Seated like royalty on the afghan covering her lap was Patches.

"Is this space taken?" Betsy asked, indicating a setting at the table with no chair.

"We saved it especially for you," Charlotte said. "Who is your handsome companion?"

"This is Patches," Betsy said. "He was recently orphaned, and I lost my dear Maltese, Skipper, before the retreat. We're both deciding whether adoption is right for us, but I have a feeling it will work out fine."

Patches gazed up at Betsy with pure adoration in his puppy eyes. He glanced away briefly to check out newcomers Lois and Reynard, who was calmer than Faith had seen him during the entire conference. Reynard didn't even bark when Jeremiah took a seat between the women, the tiny brown owl perched on his shoulder. Rose and Damian arrived, holding hands.

After everyone had settled in at the table, the questions began. Everyone had heard about the excitement at the garden shed, but few knew the facts about the heirloom seeds. Rumor had created some lively theories.

As her father answered questions, the clues to Lionel's murder fell into place, just like in some of Faith's favorite mystery novels.

"So Hannah poisoned herself?" Rose asked.

Her father nodded. "Hannah was attempting to draw suspicion away from herself. She got the idea for the poison from Lois's novel and found a picture and instructions for concocting the poison in an old book."

"My book!" Jeremiah exclaimed.

"Which you'll get back after the investigation is complete," Dad assured him. "Thankfully, she didn't dispose of it. The police found it in the trunk of her car."

"How did Hannah know where my book was?" Jeremiah asked.

"She overheard me telling you the book was in the library," Faith answered. "Remember how she bumped into me leaving the panel Wednesday? She was in a rush to go steal your book."

Jeremiah nodded. "Did you tell the police about the disturbed plant we saw in the woods?"

"Yes. They might ask you to show them where it was," Faith said. "If Watson hadn't led us to Hannah, we might never have solved the crime or recovered the things she stole. I had already learned she didn't get a ride to her farm from Glenn at the time of the murder. She used him as her alibi, knowing he was out of state on a fishing trip."

"How would she know that?" Rose asked. "I didn't even know there was a boathouse."

"While I watched the front desk for departing guests," Charlotte said, "the clerk told me Hannah had asked about taking a boat out. Perhaps she was hoping to dispose of the bloody hoe by dumping it in the ocean. But the clerk informed her that Glenn was on vacation."

"Instead, she dropped the murder weapon behind a flower planter near the gardening shed," Faith broke in. "A guest found it and thought it was a hidden treasure."

"Hannah also admitted that she put the gardening gloves in your tote bag, Lois," her father added. "She was trying to make sure the police suspected you so they wouldn't check her out thoroughly."

"I didn't help myself any," Lois said. "My tirade about Lionel must have made me sound bitter enough to kill. In the end, his bad review didn't stop my series from being extended by the publisher. I wish I could take back my words. Especially considering what happened to him."

"You had a solid alibi for the time of the murder," Faith said. "My aunt confirmed your volunteer work in Glynde. The police might not have considered you their prime suspect if you'd let them know."

"I don't like to brag about my volunteer work," Lois said. "It might be seen as a marketing scheme when I'm really just passionate about encouraging children to read." She shook her head. "My modesty almost became my undoing."

"Did you discover where the secret passage in the room led?" Faith asked Damian and Rose.

"We followed it to a storage closet full of cleaning supplies," Damian said. "Hannah used the hidden passage to gain access to my room and switch the envelopes."

"Decades ago, the passage behind the bookcase in the suite served as a route for servants to discreetly enter the room to clean," Charlotte explained.

"The talk about Castleton Manor must have inspired Hannah to do her own exploring," Faith said. "She wasn't staying here because she lives locally, but as a retreat speaker, no one questioned her wandering around the manor. And I think that wraps up all the mysteries."

"One mystery hasn't been solved," her mother said. "The sixth treasure hasn't been found."

"I thought the other five treasures were too easily discovered," Rose said. "So I made the last one more difficult."

"I don't suppose you could give us a hint?" her father asked.

"To the man who solved the murder mystery?" Rose laughed. "That would be cheating."

"There is one other mystery that won't be solved," Faith said. "We'll never know how valuable the heirloom seeds might have been to modern gardeners."

"There's hope." Dad locked eyes with Damian, and a little desperation crept into his voice. "Right?"

"The paper grocery bag was scorched and wet," Damian said. "But the seeds were inside envelopes, which were inside a manila envelope. Watson dragged the paper bag out of Hannah's car and onto the driveway before it became soaked through. The inner envelopes were dry."

"How do you know all the details?" Faith asked.

Her father's grim expression broke into a broad grin. "I convinced Chief Garris that placing the seeds in evidence storage might mean the loss of a national treasure."

"I don't think you exaggerated their importance," Damian said. "That is, if they're viable."

The group fell silent for a few moments.

Rose reached for Damian's hand. "Tell them your good news."

"With your permission, Mr. Jaxon?" Damian asked.

"Absolutely," Wolfe said.

"Castleton Manor is sponsoring my research project that will test the seeds' viability and propagate the resulting plants, if any."

"The potential scientific value of the Newberry seeds is impossible to calculate in dollars," Wolfe added.

Her father beamed. "I'm pleased to donate the seeds for the benefit of mankind."

Everyone at the table gave their congratulations.

Rose stood. "Excuse me. I have to attend to my retreat duties."

The room of chatting guests fell silent when Rose stepped behind the podium.

Rose made a few announcements. The usual thanks and awards were presented to various guests, speakers, and organizers. "Many of you may have heard about the discovery of a treasure of immeasurable value. Watson Newberry found a cache of garden seeds brought to New England in the 1800s by an ancestor of the Castleton Manor librarian." She smiled. "Watson, will you please join me?"

Faith carried Watson, debonair in clean fur and green bow tie, to the podium.

"In *The Secret Garden*," Rose continued, "Mary Lennox discovered a garden that had been hidden for ten years. Watson discovered a Secret Garden that was hidden for over a century. The Hidden Treasures Literary and Gardening Retreat presents this plaque to Watson Newberry in recognition of what may be one of the greatest discoveries of heirloom seeds in recent years."

The audience erupted in applause and cheers, and a few even jumped to their feet in a standing ovation.

Watson purred, taking all the attention in stride.

When the dessert and coffee had been finished, a few guests lingered on the loggia or strolled through the surrounding gardens. The manor would soon empty of guests until the next event.

Wolfe held Faith's hand and led her down the steps into the garden.

"Peace and quiet," she said with a sigh.

"This has been an unusually busy week," Wolfe said. "You should consider taking the next few weeks off."

"So I can prepare for the wedding?" she asked. "I think our mothers have the planning well in hand."

Wolfe shrugged. "Maybe so you can hide from the preparations."

"Don't tempt me," Faith said. "I'd rather work. Staying busy is my coping mechanism. And I can't imagine you taking a leave of absence from work."

"True. Perhaps that is part of what makes us so well suited for each other." Wolfe stopped beneath a rose arbor. "And then there's the fact that you are a beautiful woman who has captivated me with your charm."

He kissed her, and all else was forgotten.

But the moment didn't last long.

A loud whoop of delight sounded from the other side of the arbor.

"I found it!" her father exclaimed. "The sixth treasure."

Faith and Wolfe left their secluded spot to join their mothers and the guests crowding close to her dad. He looked triumphant as he grasped the handles of a picnic basket.

"What's inside?" Mom asked.

Dad set the basket on a bench and lifted the flaps, then pulled out bottles and tissue-wrapped books. "A jar of local honey. Two bottles of balsamic vinegar and two bottles of cooking oil infused with herbs from the manor's garden." He unwrapped the books. "A recipe book using ingredients you can grow in your own garden. An illustrated copy of *The Secret Garden*. Oh, and this one is by Jeremiah Fielding. *The Simple Life*, subtitled *The Quiet Enjoyment of Outdoor Spaces Large and Small*."

Wolfe leaned close to Faith and whispered, "*The Simple Life*. That sounds like a book we can both use."

A week later, the book club met in the Candle House Library. It was the first time they all had a chance to get together since the retreat ended.

Faith only had enough time to nibble on a cookie and take a sip of tea before the ladies bombarded her with questions about the mystery of Lionel's murder and the status of the heirloom seeds.

Her father had donated the seeds to the manor's sponsored project to test their viability. They were potentially very valuable, and that made him comfortable with the idea that he didn't need to shoulder the entire expense for the wedding her mother and Charlotte had planned.

"A lot hinges on whether the seeds sprout," Eileen reminded them. "They're over a hundred years old."

Midge leaned forward on her seat, holding Atticus securely on her lap. "Have you heard anything from Damian?"

"Not yet." Faith shook her head. "I'm afraid if nothing sprouts, Dad will start feeling anxious about his contribution to the wedding again."

Brooke regarded the cookie on her plate. "I can't believe Hannah poisoned herself. What a dangerous thing to do."

"After the guest found the hoe Hannah used to hit Lionel, she must have felt like the police were closing in on her," Midge said. "She was desperate."

Watson jumped off Faith's lap and sat down in the center of the circle.

"Yes, Watson," Faith said. "You were closing in on her too."

He gave her a smug look.

Eileen glanced up from her knitting. "Did Hannah confess to murdering Lionel?"

Faith nodded. "She was arguing with Lionel near the generator, and she picked up the hoe and struck him. When he fell on the generator, she opened the hopper and allowed the methane fumes to kill him."

"That's terrible," Midge said.

"I think I'm done with terrible things for a while," Faith said. "Can we talk about the novel now?"

Her friends obliged.

Faith had slipped gratefully into the carefree discussion when her cell phone chimed. She didn't want to be rude, but most of her friends were in the book group, and she had called her mother before leaving her cottage. Fearing an emergency, she checked her phone. "It's a text from Rose."

"What does she say?" Midge asked.

The book group ladies had all befriended the retreat director, and they were delighted the horticultural group had elected to return to the manor next year.

"She says she's sending a photo." Faith waited for a moment. A second text popped up. "Wow."

"What is it?" Brooke asked.

Green leaves poked above the soil in a flat of growing medium. "From Damian's lab." Faith turned the screen to face the rest of the group. "'Melissa officinalis,' Rose writes. 'Lemon balm. It sprouted.'"

Watson meowed.

"We know you discovered the seeds," Brooke said with a grin. "Good job."

Watson hopped onto Faith's lap. He reached up with his paw and patted her gently on the cheek.

Faith wrapped him in a hug. "You're a hero."

Midge reached inside her bag. "I think Watson would rather have one of these than verbal praise." She handed Faith a bag of tunaroons.

The women laughed as Watson munched a treat, then curled up on Faith's lap, purring.

Faith scratched her cat behind the ears. "Watson is so special. Most cats would go through a hole in the wall to catch a mouse. Mine goes through a hole in a wall and finds a hidden treasure."

"A secret garden," Eileen said.

Faith smiled at the thought of Watson discovering a secret garden. She hoped that someday she would be able to plant Josiah Newberry's heirloom seeds in one of the beautiful gardens at the manor, letting her ancestor's legacy live on and flourish.

As the others discussed the next book club selection, Faith felt an overwhelming gratefulness for their friendship and support. They had solved many mysteries together, and they would continue to do so.

In the meantime, Faith looked forward to exchanging vows with Wolfe and beginning the exciting new chapter in their lives, with her faithful cat by her side.

YOUR FEEDBACK MEANS A LOT TO US!

Up to this point, we've been doing all the writing. Now it's *your* turn!

Tell us what you think about this book, the characters, the bad guy, or anything else you'd like to share with us about this series. We can't wait to hear from *you*!

Log on to give us your feedback at:
https://www.surveymonkey.com/r/CastletonLibrary

Annie's FICTION